NEFERTITI

Dov Bahat

NEFERTITI

When Nefertiti, the Egyptian Queen,
met the American General "Ike" Eisenhower

Historical Novel

Astrolog Publishing House

NEFERTITI
When Nefertiti, the Egyptian Queen,
met the American General "Ike" Eisenhower
By **Dov Bahat**

Editor: Elisha Ben Mordechai
Language Consultant: Jody Baron

© Astrolog Publishing House 2014

P. O. Box 1123, Hod Hasharon 45111, Israel
TEL. 972-9-7412044
FAX. 972-9-7442714
E-Mail: abooks@bezeqint.net
e9b8m7@gmail.com
Astrolog Web Site: www.astrolog-publishing

IPG: www.ipgbook.com/
ISBN 10: 9654943522
ISBN 13: 978-9654943529

Published by Astrolog Publishing House 2014

Table of Contents

The Central Characters

Nefertiti, Queen of Egypt

Amenhotep IV – Akhenaton, King of Egypt

Ror – Thutmose, Artist of the King's Court

*Doctor Martin Klopstock, Archeologist,
employee of the Berlin Museum*

Clara, Wife of Dr. Klopstock

Chapter One:

A Celebration in Thebes

Ror and the members of his family put on their holiday best and joined the throng of people that crowded along both sides of the main thoroughfare in Thebes. The boulevard ran across the entire capitol – starting in the backstreets, and ending on the opposite side of the metropolis, in front of the king's palace. Residents from all walks of life in the great city gathered in their respective quarters, as did the family of Ror, taking its place in the city's workers' quarter along the main street. It was the king's birthday, and the magnificent procession was about to begin. While there had already been a delay of more than an hour and a half, the long wait standing in the hot sun of early spring did not bother those assembled. On the contrary. This was a festive occasion for meeting many acquaintances and being seen in one's finest clothing. When someone tired of standing for an extended time in one spot, they would move to another place and mingle among more friends.

It was the children's joy especially that created the atmosphere of celebration. They ran about with fun and mischief, playing hide-and-seek with one another. Here and there they would grab "bargains" from the kiosks of the hawkers, for whom this was a big day. The children's favorite holiday treat was the amardine, made by stamping with bare feet on apricot fruit that had been soaked in sugar cane juice and flattened. In this way the masses could be like their admired queen, who everyone knew loved to sip the apricot nectar brought to her by the king's servants whenever she wished. The amardine was not just to eat. It served as a substance for massaging the skin. The children's mothers believed that the apricot prevented wrinkles on the skin of the neck and that it preserved the smoothness of the skin of Queen Nefertiti's face. Although purchase of the expensive apricot nectar was beyond the means of the working class women, the desire for the amardine was such that they urged and encouraged their children to obtain enough for them as well, to taste after and between their meals, as well as to use for other purposes.

And now the drums were heard, their sound coming closer and getting louder, and then the trumpets' blast, so pleasing to the ear, became amplified. The children kept running about but the adults began to settle in and find places they would remain in for the duration of the coming parade.

The king's birthday was of special importance – and festivity prevailed among the nation's masses. Everyone was supposed to dance and rejoice on this special day intended for joy. This festival was in direct contrast to other holidays in the kingdom, which were centered around the concept of the continuation of those departing from this world on their way to the next. Such was the convention in ancient Egypt with respect to all that had to do with the official funeral customs dedicated to death and to the deceased who arrived in heaven embalmed and mummified. Mummification expressed the lofty achievements of medical science. The magnificent burial monuments demonstrated the peak of engineering knowledge of those times and they contained the greatest artistic works of antiquity.

On this day of celebration the populace felt the power of their country. The parade began with the holy procession of the priests. The most important of the religious priests customarily appeared with their High Priest marching in front. The priests' garments were pure white, made of linen knitted from the fibers of the flax plant. This fabric was considered highest quality as it held up in the face of the sun's rays and constant and repeated laundering due to its long fibers.

The linen that draped the priests was of the finest sort. The sharp eyes of Ror's mother did not fail to take in the considerable difference between the garments of the priests passing by her, and her own.

The gold jewelry adorning the priests' bodies glistened in the sunlight – representing power, strength, and rule. Gold was also seen as having healing and magical qualities as well as powers to protect against the evil eye and to promote health and happiness. The priests used it to display their strength, their authority, and their wealth. To the country's loyal believers gold symbolized the body of the god Ra.

So began the festivities, with every priest worthy of

his station taking part in the splendid annual event. As the religious leaders passed by the crowds, their sharp eyes watched their countrymen bow deeply, foreheads touching the ground as the legs of the priests strode past.

At a considerable distance from the procession of priests the great Egyptian army made its way forward. The time that lapsed between one procession and the next gave the crowd a chance to rise up from their submissive kneeling before the clergy, and to stand up straight to greet with appropriate cheer the army so loved by the simple people.

First, the various infantry units marched by. The crowd greeted the mighty bodies of the soldiers with shouts of awe and appreciation. The people had come mostly from the impoverished streets of the country where there was not always enough food on the table for every member of the family, and they were often hungry. It was known that when skinny youths went into army service they would put on weight and become stronger as a result of the board they received during their training for war. The beaming soldiers displayed their modern weapons with pride: swords and shields made of animal skins stretched on wooden frames, and bows and arrows. The officers grasped short daggers made of bronze that had recently become a standard weapon of the army.

The crowd of citizens paid special respect to the cavalry riding in splendid glory on the famous horses of Egypt. In those days, the number and quality of its horses was the measure of any respectable nation, and the might of the Egyptian cavalry was renowned. The horsemen's shields were made of solid wood and covered with bronze that gleamed in the sunlight. The tips of their spears were also made of bronze. These glistening tools of war were proof to the nation of the cavalry soldiers' preferred status over that of the infantrymen.

Each year the climax of the parade was the arrival of the chariots. The sound of the chariots cast an enchanted spell on the spectators. The commotion that erupted from the wheels and merged with the sounds made by the galloping hooves of the horses intoxicated the crowds, especially when joined by the neighing of the horses, sounding as if they were orchestrated by the military commanders. Each chariot carried "young heroes", one being the driver of the horse or horses (according to the tactical purpose the chariot served), and the second being the archer, whose skill at hitting enemy soldiers was the deciding factor in the fate of any battle. The chariot personnel drew adoration and applause from the people, and voices rose and intensified along with the increasing blasts of the trumpets and the thundering of the drums. The people accepted with understanding and affection the piles of droppings left behind along the entire main avenue of the city by the cavalry and by the clangorous horses harnessed to the chariots, just as loving mothers accept all that is involved in the care of an infant that does not yet control his functions.

The new innovations evident in this part of the procession made up most of the talk the next day in the streets of the capitol, along with the delighted comments of the women who praised the good looks of the officers' uniforms.

However, on this special day of celebration another highlight stood out – one that was presented to the people as a surprise. This year, the king did not make do with the traditional procession. Among the throngs the rumor was passed that at the end of the military parade the king's open chariot would carry his queen, Nefertiti, the most beautiful among women. Only a few days before had this sensational information been announced, intensifying the excitement leading up to the big event.

The populace received with shouts of "Hail the queen!" the wonderful sight of the woman renowned as the "most beautiful woman in the world." She sat in complete radiance in the large golden chariot and waved to the crowd that looked to her to be mesmerized. This was the day the populace was told that "if one drinks to intoxication, that is to be praised". She liked seeing the people happy and that happiness increased her enjoyment of the divine reception she was awarded from them. The golden chariot passed slowly among the throngs and everyone blinked at the radiant woman in an effort to capture her beauty in their glance.

Nefertiti's nakedness was concealed by a light cover made of knitted linen of purest white that flowed from her shoulders all the way to her feet. The queen was known to have a strong affinity for gold jewelry. On her head on top of a wig of smooth black hair rose a golden bonnet set with rows of blue stones of lapis lazuli and green fragments of faience glass. On her breast hung a large and splendid gold necklace in the center of which shone a bronze plate. In the middle of the plate, as large as an ostrich egg, was set a blue lapis lazuli crystal. The queen's right arm was covered from wrist to elbow with a gold armlet on which was engraved the name of the king along with the name of the queen, while her left arm was adorned with gold bracelets.

Only a few of the citizens were able to see her face on account of the glare radiating from the surface of the shining chariot and penetrating their eyes. Nor did many manage to perceive her waves of greeting through the cloud of dust that rose from the wheels of the royal vehicle. In spite of this, when she passed the place where each person stood applauding and bowing, they knew with certainty that beauty such as this had never been seen before. Especially emotional were the women and girls, and some of them lost their equilibrium as they shouted out loud "Hail, hail the queen!" It was an experience never to be forgotten by the excited women.

At the end of the procession, the King held a reception at the entrance to the palace for senior members of the priesthood and the military officers, attended by the queen. Not all of the aristocrats took part in the reception due to lack of sufficient room in the inner palace courtyard. The honored guests reached the inner court after passing through a gate in the outer wall. They went along the central path that divided the collection of buildings arranged symmetrically around the palace. The flags of the kingdom and the army flew atop the wall around the courtyard. The rectangular floor was covered with tiles of rough shale brought from Sinai, creating an illusion of a vast carpet that bestowed honor on those who stood upon it during the distinguished ceremony.

The reception ceremony, which took place at high noon, was short, so as not to cause the participants too much suffering. First, the High Priest stood facing the king and queen and read from a parchment the declaration of loyalty – his own and the priests' – to the king. Next, the army commander fell to his knees and bowed his head. He then got to his feet and pronounced the pledge of the army to the monarchy. The king responded with his acceptance, in his own name and in the name of the God Sun, the declaration of loyalty of the priests and the oath of the army. With that, the ceremony was complete.

The majority of country's citizens did not attend the reception in the palace courtyard, so they heard about the important event from whispered hearsay in the days and weeks following the king's birthday. On the evening of the magnificent parade the people had family parties celebrating the auspicious day. Ror's family gathered with their neighbors in the front courtyard shared by their clay houses, in one of the alleyways of the workers' quarter. Date wine and sweet foodstuffs made of sugar cane were generously shared among the gathered, and everyone was busy relaying stories of what they had experienced on that day of celebration. The elders told of the king's birthday celebrations in earlier years, and they pointed out with satisfaction that today's event had surpassed the beauty of those that preceded it. The youngsters were very impressed by the military presence in the parade and they vowed to themselves and to the others that in the future, when they grew up, they too would participate in the infantry march or the ride of the cavalry, or if they were really fortunate, they would appear as chariot heroes, soldiers of the King. Little Rora, when asked if she had enjoyed the procession, considered how to respond, and then answered that she had not known that horses could leave so many droppings in the street...

Chapter Two:
Hail the New King

The residents of the workers' quarter in which Ror grew up did not have a lot to say about the nature of the new religion that was coming into being before their eyes. Neither were they very interested in the changes taking place in their city as long as every man was provided with work that brought his family sustenance, however meager. Ror had a good mother. She managed to finish her housework before his father arrived in the evening from his job, and in the free time left to her she would talk with Ror, the eldest son in the family, about the future. She was not an educated woman, but she understood that education was the key to a better future, and she urged Ror to do all he could to change the course of his life so as not to continue until old age doing the same work that supplied the livelihood of his father. It would be best, she explained to him, to try achieving "something more promising".

From the darkness before dawn until the darkness after sunset, Ror's father carried heavy boulders to be used in the building and expansion of the new city. He often returned with injured hands, and Ror's mother would be called upon to bandage and administer to his wounds. She gathered special plants for this purpose from small inlets along the great river.

It was clear to all the members of the family that

the mother's lofty and expansive aspirations would be impossible to attain, since, of course, a laborer always remained a laborer, and the continuous social hierarchy was what would decide for the next generation – and for all the generations to come – who would be rich and who would remain poor all his life. Everyone knew that the interesting jobs, those that did not involve the hoisting of heavy rocks onto one's back or shoulders, were given only to the wealthy who were able to acquire the appropriate training for desirable positions and had the right connections at their disposal.

From the day that Ror joined the ranks of the workers in the great quarry, he held a burning desire to impress the work manager in charge in hopes that an opening to advancement, however narrow, might be afforded him. In contrast to most of the laborers working along with him, who marched in long lines with heavy loads on their backs and saw only the bare, lacerated feet of those walking ahead of them, Ror tried to observe everything taking place around him and to imprint it all in his mind, in hopes that perhaps some of it would be helpful to him one day.

As he worked, the experience he acquired taught him that while the stones mostly looked identical one to another, when examined more closely, significant differences in their shapes became apparent. It turned out that some of the rock pieces piled in the quarry, those about the size of a medium-sized watermelon, were shapeless and had protrusions and hollow spaces, whereas there were other pieces of rock that resembled the shape of a brick. Clearly any builder would prefer to work with stones having an even geometric shape that would facilitate the building of a wall with no protrusions or cavities. Precision with regard to proportions in the structure would significantly improve its stability. When Ror studied in more depth the walls of the quarry from which building materials were being mined, he discovered to his surprise that the cubical stones were arranged next to one another in particular layers of the rock, whereas other layers sere made up of pieces of shapeless boulder lacking geometric proportions.

Today, we can explain the phenomenon that Ror discovered in the stone using basic theories of geology. Geological pressures applied in particular directions to the rock, formed straight cracks in some of the layers and cut the stones into pieces resembling bricks, and in other layers this did not occur. Three thousand years ago the same physical laws that we are now familiar with affected the rock, but the theory had not yet been formulated. Ror, truth be told, did not need complicated theories. He made do with the interesting information with which he could demonstrate that different layers of rock in the walls of the quarry behaved in different ways with respect to the provision of raw materials for the erection of buildings in the city.

Deciding to take a chance, Ror pointed out his observations to the work overseer. The overseer was impressed by what he was shown. Several days later,

Ror was informed that it had been decided that he was to receive a bigger ration of meat, and also that his salary would be raised. Later, he was told that his overseer had passed on the fascinating information about the differentiation between the layers of rock most appropriate for use in building and those less useful, to his superiors. The superiors had examined Ror's ideas, and found them to be correct. As a result, Ror's overseer had been promoted in rank and appointed as manager of a larger group of laborers.

At Ror's home happiness abounded. He bought a new pair of sandals for his father and for his mother he bought a lovely colorful sash. Among the engineers, the rumor circulated that Ror's overseer had discovered an improved process of mining the quarry, but among the workers everyone knew that Ror was the great discoverer. While there were some administrative snafus, it seemed the boulders in the limestone quarries of ancient Egypt could speak, and Ror's good name became well known among the management. His special talents were recognized, and he was added to the engineering staff of the quarry. He was assigned the task of marking the walls of the quarry, indicating the layers that were likely to be productive when mined for raw building material, in order to distinguish them from the layers that would not be productive and in which it would not be worthwhile to invest labor.

In due course, the hours that Ror actually labored were shortened, and the time he spent in thought was increased. He considered what his steps would be in the future, while remembering his past and where he came from. He and his family, and thousands of other laborers and their families were moved by order of the king from the old capitol city, Thebes, to a new place in the desolate desert, in order to build a new city. The king named the new city "Akhenaton". In the old city Ror had been a member of a family of workers that had always been able to earn their livelihoods. However, many others did not have permanent sources of income. In the new city, blessed be the king, there would be plentiful work for everyone.

Those moving from one city to the next naturally made comparisons, since everything was different. Until houses were built in the new city, most of the families had to live on the sands of the desert. They spread papyrus mats, above them and on the ground, as protection from the winds. Papyrus was abundantly found along the banks of the River of Egypt and in the inlet pools that surrounded it. With this plant one could make almost anything: "From this reed Yocheved wove Moses' basket" was the legend that spread by word of mouth among the laborers. It could be put into use for warmth during the cold nights of winter to lesson the suffering of the family members. "The situation will spur them to work quickly", said the senior overseers to the engineers, "so they can get into houses as soon as possible."

Of course, the laborers would live in houses made

of clay, so some of them were put to work in the clay. However, many were assigned hard labor with huge boulders where there was a need, and with smaller stones in other places, all in order to build the palaces of the royal family and other shrines. Members of the higher classes also would have the right to live in stone houses.

The heads of the king and his wife the queen were filled with thoughts. In particular, the young king would never forget a particular day. Before he was crowned, he took part in a long boat trip on the great river, in order to know better the towns and villages along its shores. As he went from place to place he discovered the beauty of his land. At each site, when he landed and went ashore, the masses greeted him with honor and respect. Everyone knew the prince was soon to become king, and heartfelt smiles full of admiration were offered to him with love. In every hamlet he visited, his eyes were met by the sight of many adoring faces, hands waving, and mouths calling out words of blessing.

During the days and nights of that voyage the prince focused his thoughts on his future and the future of the kingdom. At the end of that particular night, a blazing fire broke out on the main deck of the boat. The winds stormed around it and the flames rose to the top of the mast, but the boat was not burned and the deck was not consumed. A voice came from the fire: "My son, my son, pay respects to me in the desert in full light at my new tabernacle." Then the fire subsided a bit. Suddenly the flames got bigger and the voice returned: "My son, my son, pay respects to me in the desert in full light at my new tabernacle." The prince was filled with fear and fell prostrate, trembling before the fire, his face pressed to the boards of the deck and his hands spread in front of him. The voice repeated: "My son, my son, pay respects to me in the desert in full daylight at my new tabernacle." When the prince lifted his face the fire had vanished and it was as if it had never been. The prince looked around and saw that none of his servants or officers was on the deck. All of them were deeply asleep in their cabins in the belly of the boat. Then the prince understood what the Sun God had ordered him "in full light": That he relocate the capitol to the desert, far away from Thebes, and that there he was to build a new shrine. The prince then turned his attention to the changes he would make in the religion. His father had reinforced the power of the priests, and they in turn had used the faith of the people as leverage for gaining political strength and economic fortune. They were not involved in spiritual work, but rather they engaged in shamefully taking advantage of their followers. He would get rid of the religion that worshiped false gods and would establish a single deity, the authentic god, the Sun disk. The treacherous religion of Amon would be replaced by the worship of the all-inspiring Aton.

His wife, his love, Nefertiti, had not accompanied him on this sailing journey. Therefore he was spared a lot of laughter, entertainment, and affection and was able to devote himself to the ideological development of his new vision.

Returning from the voyage, as he approached his home port of Thebes the prince saw a multitude of vessels approaching his ship. Some of them were small papyrus boats without sails, making their way using oars, and others had triangular sails. Most impressive were the large wooden yachts sporting triangular sails and gigantic masts. The smaller boats deferred to the larger ones as they made their way toward the prince's vessel. The people in the smaller boats noticed that the important personages on thc larger ones stood at attention in imitation of the statues they were familiar with from the holy temples.

The High Priest Aye and the adjutants attending him on the prince's ship made their cumbersome way toward the wide deck. They were weighty men who looked quite different from the gaunt citizenry. Gold bracelets surrounded their forearms and bound their hands and elbows like shackles. They fell in prostrate submission at the prince's feet and he regarded them with astonishment. The sun, in all its intensity, lit up the earth and sky. He looked upward and then looked back, his eyes unable to withstand the powerful rays.

The clamor subsided and silence fell. Only the sound of the peaceful gentle waves on the river was heard in the background.

The prince knew that the great day had arrived. His father, Amenhotep III, had gone to the next world, and in just a short time he, the prince, would be named Amenhotep IV. His keen ear picked up isolated premature shouts of "Hail the new king!" He knew that soon, when he heard the words "hail the king" coming from the masses, they would be directed at him.

When the prince arrived at the palace and passed through the gate in the outer wall, his mother, Tiye, came out to greet him. Her forehead touched the carpet of bulrushes that was spread between the outer and inner gates. She did not raise her head from the floor until he approached her, wrapped her in his slender, gentle arms, and lifted her up. Her head remained bent toward his chest and she waited. Fears gnawed at her heart. She had reason for the doubts that played in her mind.

As a child, Amenhotep had often played with scarabs fashioned by his father in the shape of a type of the dung beetle. There were many different kinds of dung beetles, and the most admired in the eyes of Amenhotep III and his priests was the "Pharaoh's dung beetle". They believed these insects to be holy, due to the beetle's emergence from the dung, which they saw as symbolic of "creating something from nothing" – a godly deed. These scarabs were common in the streets of the kingdom, carved from stone and made from clay and other materials. Adults used them as tiny amulets, adornments, and seals, and they served as toys and entertainment for the prince growing up in the palace, before he became the king.

It is true that during the reign of Amenhotep III the

religion of Amon was dominant in Egypt. However, to a certain extent, and with his secret encouragement, there were also rustlings of the religion of Aton.

Growing up, the prince did not like his mother, Tiye. She did not approve of the games he played with the scarabs supplied by his nursemaid, as they insulted the religion of Amon. When he came of age, the prince became aware of how his mother was responsible for the cultivation of the religious priests. She controlled them, and reinforced their power. His father waged wars against enemies outside the borders of the kingdom, while she took part in games of hierarchy that enlarged her influence. The prince felt that his mother tried to stand in the way of his rise to greatness, since Tiye, the mother, favored his eldest brother, who had been destined to be his father's heir when the time came, as was accepted practice in those days. Fate would have it, however, that the eldest brother was afflicted an ailment from which he did not recover, and his younger sibling, assuming his place, became Amenhotep IV.

The embalming of a dead king played a central role in the culture of ancient Egypt, and the funeral activity lasted seventy days and nights. These were days of mourning in the City of Amon, during which the serving spigots of the "drink that brings joy to the human heart" were closed in all the taverns, and no fine-figured dancing women were seen in the saloons. Instead, professional weepers could be heard wailing and crying. The more they cried, the more they were paid.

In the Egyptian Empire the belief was held that a person being was comprised of two parts, the physical and the spiritual. The first was defined as the human body, and the second was comprised of the soul, and according to this apportionment, it was thought that the emotions resided in the heart. When a person died, the soul was liberated from the body and began its own journey. In order to sustain the soul in its wanderings, it was necessary to equip it with food and drink. This is why pottery vessels were placed at the side of each mummy in its tomb, containing provisions for the path of unknown destination. The spirit leaving the body needed a permanent residence to which it could return in time, when the dead came back to life. The better the quality of the embalmment and the preservation of the corpse, the more beneficial to the fate of the soul when it returned. These beliefs made up the foundation for mummification playing such an important part in Egyptian cultural practice.

The physicians who executed the sacred craft of mummification enjoyed a special rank in the nation. Their professional expertise was passed down in families from father to son, and a special semi-mythical aura surrounded the elite embalmers. They were even more respected than the priests, though also more despised, since they were seen as desecrating the holy bodies of the deceased. The embalmers naturally developed different levels of quality of mummification; this in accordance with the monetary contribution the client was willing to invest in the preservation of the corpse.

Unexpectedly, Amenhotep IV demanded to take part in the mummification of his father after his death. Clearly, this was a most repulsive activity – only a few could withstand the sights and the smells that accompanied the embalming process. Those involved at first refused to allow the designated king to be present as they worked, but his insistence overcame their refusal. The young prince made sure to be present for the duration of the mummification and to observe the entire complicated operation. Doing this made him shine yet brighter in the eyes of Nefertiti, his wife, and showed her how complex a person her husband was. Thutmose, the sculptor who will be told about shortly, was impressed as well by the fortitude and bravery of Amenhotep IV, his king, who in the eyes of many was a weakling who lacked courage, since it was known that he was not a lover of war or battle.

The embalming process began with the removal of the brain by way of the nostrils. This was carried out with the use of a hook made of flexible copper metal, allowing the execution of complicated operations within the scull of the corpse. The brain was rinsed with date wine, treated with perfume, and then dried. Afterwards it was stored in a special vessel that was kept apart from the other body parts. In order to prevent decay in the skull cavity that had been emptied, it was filled with perfumed embalming herbs and then sealed by closing off the nostrils with linen plugs. The main incision in the body was made along its side, and through it by way of additional incisions; the various organs of the chest and abdomen were removed. They received the same treatment as had the brain, and the lungs, kidneys, and liver were stored in separate containers. Embalming plants soaked in perfumed resins were introduced into the cavities created by the removal of the organs, and the incision on the side of the body was sutured. The body was covered with long-lasting linen shrouds. There were some periods where an attempt was made to use a replacement for linen, but Amenhotep IV insisted on a return to that fabric that for the treatment of his father's body. Each body part that was removed was placed inside a special container, alongside the food and drink that were arranged next to the body inside the tomb.

In addition to the high level of medical sophistication the ancient physicians had achieved, they also showed a great early understanding of the secrets of chemistry, without familiarity, of course, with any of the formulas that we know today. They knew well the actions of various minerals they had access to. The embalmers displayed special expertise in the use of sodium and calcium. Sodium carbonate assisted the removal of fluids from the body and sodium bicarbonate lowered the acidity, such that they prevented the multiplication of germs and the creation of decay in the body of the deceased. The ancient doctors were also familiar with the medicinal value of cooking salt and whitewash (calcium oxide), which assisted them in the craft of embalming.

The king's funeral was one of the biggest that the Egyptian kingdom had ever known. The people loved their king, under whose reign the nation had achieved great prosperity. Not even the officials knew the real wealth and borders of the kingdom, since these expanded each time the king returned from his battles. During the time of Amenhotep III the realm of the Egyptian dynasty reached northward to Syria, and to the south it penetrated deeply into Sudan. Even the desert to the east of the Nile and the coast of the Red Sea, which included half of the Sinai peninsula, were included within the borders of the kingdom. The desert to the west of the Nile – "The Great River of Egypt" – and the oases scattered within it, were part of the king's property.

When the funeral week ended, in the Valley of the Kings there arose a new king to rule – Amenhotep IV. This was a king who believed in one god and understood the principle of equality. Of course, true equality cannot be achieved in a monarchy. However, a reasonable reduction of the gaps within the kingdom was definitely possible. He was disturbed by the inflated hierarchy of his father's time. His mother glorified the hierarchy and helped those seeking authority to be strengthened. He immediately announced that his wife, Queen Nefertiti, would have rights equal to his own, and the crown on her head was of the same size at his own crown.

Under the rule of Amenhotep III, ancient Egyptian culture had prospered and reached its zenith, by judicious control and oversight of the natural and human resources at its disposal, under the rule of a single sovereign, the god-like Pharaoh who ruled the kingdom with no restraints. Egypt developed controlled irrigation of the fertile Nile Valley, and made advances in everything having to do with agriculture. Egypt was successful at deriving minerals from the desert region and its surroundings, and used its military victories and the widening of the areas in its control to bring abundant trade and very large profits. The wide use of slaves made it possible to achieve unprecedented wealth, admired and envied by every state in the ancient world.

It was under these conditions that the bureaucracy evolved, being based upon the contributions of enlightened scribes and powerful local governors. The advancement assisted in the development of the language, writing, literature, and the arts, of which the crowning glory was the art of sculpture – the carving and the painting. The stems of the papyrus reeds, growing mostly along the banks of the waterways, held a special role, since it was upon them that the Egyptians produced papyrus scrolls. These papyri were fashioned by laying pallets of narrow strips cut from the stem of the papyrus plant laid closely side by side, slightly overlapping, so that all the strips point in the same direction. On top of this layer was lain an additional layer, with all of the strips pointing in the opposite direction to those below. In this manner a length and breadth structure was created. This double layer matt was then pressed in order to release any fluids collected within, until it was completely dried. Papyrus was found to be stable in the dry Egyptian climate, and the papyrus paper that was created using this process were used for the scrolls that were an important foundation of the Egyptian administration. Research on the extensive information that was collected on the papyri has allowed archeologists to the way of life in ancient Egypt.

The intellectual climate of ancient Egypt during the period of transfer of the monarchy was such that many questions were asked. Where had Amenhotep IV derived the ideas that created his vision on the deck of his ship? From where had the giant fire come? And what about the intense light that had whispered his fate and told him how to fashion the future of his kingdom? What had summoned the god Aton to the king's heir, and what had illuminated the prince's path as the god revealed himself on the ship?

The new king met with his staff of senior engineers, instilled them with his vision, and commanded them to make detailed plans, mainly for the swift move of the royal castles from Thebes, the old capitol in upper Egypt in the South, to central Egypt, where it was given the name "Akhetaton". At the same time, the king changed his own name to "Akhenaton". This was a political upheaval of historic proportions. "Akhenaton" established a new religion in "Akhetaton" the main precept of which was the belief in one god, "Aton". The king was his son and his representative on Earth.

When the High Priest and his adjutants came to the young king and with complaints about the changes taking place around them, he immediately dismissed them from their authority and sent some of them, those considered the most grievous transgressors, to work in the mines. The existence of the priests of the older generation constituted a threat, since they carried many secrets of the monarchy, and their loyalty to the king, after being removed from their powerful positions, became doubtful. These swift changes quickly convinced the citizens of the capitol that the old world was gone, and a new world had been created.

The evening before the day of the king's move from the old capitol to the new, the king went up to the roof of his house, wanting to be alone to say goodbye to the city of his birth that he had loved, and had also come to hate. He had the feeling that the twinkling lights of the city around him were not in agreement with his decision, but that they would accept his authority. The crescent moon revolved in the sky, and smiled down at him as a messenger of the sun, silently approving the huge change about to take place. Tomorrow would be warmer than the preceding days. Even the stars floating through the breadth of the heavens silently transmitted to him their prayer for the safe move from the old city to the new.

Akhenaton gazed for a long while at the three bright

stars he saw lined up in a row. They made up the "Belt of Orion". It was easy to identify them in the clear sky over Egypt. The Belt had been recognized by man for thousands of years and brought luck to those who knew its secrets. Akhenaton's astronomers taught him that by creating a right angle using the line of the Belt and the line going to the adjoining star (the one extending rightward from the Belt), an arrowhead was formed. Opening a sharp angle leftward relative to the north reveals the northeastern direction. In that direction, the chariot journey that would take a whole day, or two, depending on their speed, would bring him to the place where he would establish the new capitol "Akhetaton".

The astronomers informed Akhenaton that the early Sumerians who lived in southern Mesopotamia, (modern-day Iraq), saw a sheep in the Orion constellation. In Ancient Egypt, however, those same stars were associated with the god Osiris. Osiris was one of the most prominent gods in Egyptian mythology. Having the body of a man, he was the son of the God Sun Ra, lord of all the universe and king of the gods. Ra created the netherworld along with his sister Isis, and together they brought culture, abundance, and prosperity to the world. Osiris was also the god of the dead and the underworld. He judged every deceased when they entered the gates of the world of the dead.

The theological theories told to Akhenaton by his sages sounded interesting, but his soul went out to Aton. In his youth Akhenaton preferred to listen to his heart and did not follow the logic of the experienced priests. He knew that the task fell to him to create a new god.

Along with all this, how amazing it is to think that the three great pyramids in Giza stand in the same geometrical line toward the northeast, the identical direction to that of the Belt of Orion. This meant that scientists before Akhenaton's time had placed great significance on the northeast. This fact convinced the king that consideration of that constellation was worthwhile when there arose the need to make important decisions about the future of the kingdom.

Chapter Three:
The First and the Last Battle

A menhotep IV would never forget the upsetting experience that surrounded his participation in battle while yet a youth, when he set out to accompany his father, Amenhotep III. This took place during one of the important wars, when the king and his mighty army went to Syria on a campaign of conquest and suppression. It was to be the first and the last battle for the young Amenhotep IV. He was forced to take the place of his elder brother, the one designated to inherit their father's place as commander of the army and the task of expanding the kingdom when the time came, who had remained at the palace, ill and in need of medical treatment. The father understood that the elder child's infirmity would make it impossible for him to manage the future battles of the monarchy, and so it would be necessary to train his younger son for the tasks that undoubtedly awaited him in the future.

The young man did not like the journey of hardship, which his father saw as a journey of enjoyment. To make his participation in the historic event more pleasing, during the journey to Syria he was denied no indulgence to which he was accustomed back at the palace. All of his needs were taken care of with abundance and the devoted servants endeavored to cheer and delight him.

He disliked being forced to stay in the chariot all

the long days that extended into weeks. He especially hated the dust that penetrated the vehicle in which he was trapped as they crossed into the land of Canaan. None of the efforts made to seal the small openings in the chariot were successful. The dust made its way in through the tiny cracks and straight to the nose of the sensitive youth.

From time to time his father suggested that he ride with him up to the observation post in order to observe with his own eyes the personal contact of the fighters, those trying to kill one another and not to be killed. Emphasis was put on the smaller battles in which the Egyptian army's clear advantage was assured and the enemy's slaughter was swift. During this type of battle the king would draw close on his horse, almost to the front line, in order to hear the shouts of victory of his soldiers and the sighs of torment of the wounded enemy. In these cases, being wounded usually meant slow death involving much suffering.

The father was aware of his young son's delicate nature, and hoped that with maturity the youth would be able to overcome the shortcomings of his childhood. In an effort to encourage him, he spread before him the plans for the campaign. The boy showed no particular interest in the program. At the end of the unsuccessful military discussion, the father said to his son: "We'll arrive in Megiddo during this trip, and there we will remain for an extended period. You will be able to rest as you wish before we proceed to Syria."

The son was grateful to his father for showing him much consideration for the duration of the difficult journey. Megiddo was the most important city in Egypt's holdings at the time, located in the northern region of the kingdom. From here complete control was executed over the collection of taxes taken in from Canaan. In the center of the city a palace was built, around which was erected a set of royal buildings for the purpose of hosting the king, his son and his family, and the senior staff that accompanied them on their repeated visits to Canaan. The army headquarters was also here. It was in this place that the army prepared for its continued advancement each time it planned an action in Syria, in Mitanni, and in the Hittite Empire in central Turkey. Near Megiddo, military training camps and the army's main supply center were established. Megiddo was also of great ideological significance with respect to national pride, the passing on of military tradition, and the battle legacy of the much-revered Egyptian army. King Amenhotep III led the prince to army headquarters where the senior officers awaited. Everyone saluted the king and the prince with honor and respect. On the wall next to the chair of the Megiddo army commander hung a map made of parchment, and on it was illustrated the historic battle that had been led by the great pharaoh King Thutmose III against an alliance of opposing nations. King Amenhotep III described this battle to his son in every detail. In the Egyptian army every soldier who became an officer studied the history of that battle:

One hundred years earlier, a group of Canaanites had assembled, including an army dispatched from Mitanni (the kingdom residing in northern Mesopotamia, near the Turkish border). That army assembled near Megiddo and readied itself for a decisive battle against Egypt. In order to block the advancement of the Egyptians, the coalition army split into two parts and lined up along a line dividing Megiddo from the southeast to the northwest. Southeast of Megiddo they stood in the region of Ta'anakh, in anticipation of the possibility of the Egyptian army arriving from the Jezreel Valley. To the northwest, the armies halted in the area of Tel Shosh (adjacent to what is today Mishmar Ha'Emek) in order to prevent infiltration from the Zevulun Valley. The Canaanites did not close off Wadi Ara (which is the ancient Arona pass) in the southwest. In that direction, the river chiseled its way along the intersection between the hard rock of the Umm Al-Fahm mountain range and the softer rock of the valley of Ramat Menashe. Beyond that point, it was thought that the covering of thick forest would make passage impossible, and in the opinion of the Canaanite command it would not be traversed by the Egyptian chariots.

Thutmose took the risk, and he did lead his army along the difficult route, surprising the Canaanites near Megiddo. In the battle that took place the next day the Canaanite army was hit hard, and most of its chariots were destroyed or captured. After that astonishing victory the commanders were unable to control the

Egyptian soldiers' looting, and tactically, the king was not able to take advantage of his success. The city closed up behind its fortifications and the Egyptians kept it under siege for seven months, until it surrendered. This event is illustrated in the inscriptions found in the temple Thutmose III built in Karnak, which the military staff studied well. The more they could learn of the tales of that war, the better.

The young prince, however, was not at all interested in the details of the famous battle. He aspired to let off his nervous energy in a different way. And it turned out there was a solution to the frustration of the one destined to become Amenhotep IV. The thick forest that covered Mount Carmel was a paradise where most species of forest animals living in that time of antiquity could be found. The prince could not stand to see the blood of a man being shed, but he did see the hunting of beasts dangerous to humans as allowable, and even condoned by the gods. In the depths of the heavy thicket of the forest, the Egyptian army's engineering unit prepared roads wide enough for the passage of chariots, including the broad chariot of His Excellency the Prince. He was pleased to see animals unknown in Egypt crossing the path in front of him. There were stags and does, bears, rhinos, and even elephants of shorter stature than those from Africa. The prince ended the day of his big hunt with the killing of a lion, and a message was sent to his father informing him that the final thrust of the spear, that which had killed the dangerous animal, had been executed by his valiant son. For the king, this was the best and most satisfying evening since they had left their palace in Thebes.

When the army's halt in Megiddo ended and preparations were being made for the march on Syria (to carry out their main reason for the campaign), the prince went to his father and asked if he may remain in Megiddo and wait for the great army to return after it accomplished the mission for which it had set out to Syria. The prince suggested that when the king and his army came back through Megiddo on their way home to Egypt, he would rejoin them. Amenhotep did not derive any pride from this request, but he came to the realization that all things considered, it was preferable to accept his son's suggestion, under the condition of course, that someone could be found to look after him properly in his father's absence. There were many volunteers for the task, even though all were aware that if something were to befall the mischievous youth, the price to be paid would be the head of the one responsible for him. There was no refusing the king's demand, so the problem was solved, seemingly, to the satisfaction of all concerned.

The northward march of Amenhotep III, which his son had participated in and thus experienced war, did not end with ideological success. The prince was still apathetic to the battle victories of the armies of the brave king. The prince's excitement over the war, if indeed there was such, was not apparent in his facial expression when he was queried about it. However this failure in his son's education did not prevent Amenhotep III from continuing to carry out conquering expeditions in the lands to the north and the south, as were demanded by the needs of the country. After one such campaign, the king returned with a handsome woman. She was the daughter of the king of Mitanni, and the Egyptian king married her to strengthen the political ties with that northern kingdom. Based on the strengthening and fortification of the military axis between the two most important capitols of the day, an additional princess was sent from Mitanni. Younger than the previous one, this princess was designated for the prince, who in the meantime had reached his manhood. The princess was called Nefertiti. She was reared and educated in the royal house of Egypt until it was her time to rise to prominence.

King Amenhotep III was a man of great imagination, and he explored every matter in depth in order to derive from it the most benefit for the future. It was this analytical thinking that made possible his many great achievements. The archives of the kings that were discovered by archeologists in Akhetaton, after its destruction and its name was changed to "Tel Amarna" (known as "the Archive of Amarna"), contained commercial records, diplomatic letters, and documents that had come from the Egyptian governors in Canaan, the Hittite countries, Mitanni, Ashur, and Babylonia. During the period of Amenhotep III's reign

Egyptian maritime commerce expanded to international proportions, reaching northward to Syria and Canaan, and also to the south. Commerce continued to grow and develop, especially after the canal was dug that connected the Red Sea with the great river, making it possible to sail to countries along the equator.

Chapter Four:
The New City

R or's new appointments and his now select standing
- known among the citizens of "Akhetaton" – as
well as the high salary he received, made it possible for
him and his family members to move from their meager
clay dwelling in the outskirts of the city to a stone house
in its center. With their move to the new home, Ror and
his family discovered that the new city was developing a
rich and active cultural life. The cultural dynamic of the
city surpassed even the momentum of its construction.
This culture of Ancient Egypt came to life and was fed
by the new religion that was coming into being, and it
placed art at its center. Ror, now belonging to the middle
class, discovered that he possessed abilities and talents
he could not have realized as a member of the laboring
class, while he also discovered that along with his
new privileges came certain religious responsibilities.
Of course the right to choose to what extent he would
accept the new culture, or conversely, to what extent he
would not make it part of his own or his family's life,
was denied him completely.

Ror was thrust into the new cultural life by the
well-oiled administrative system, and he understood
right away that the faster he learned the essence of the
religious changes going on before his eyes, the better
it would be for him, and the more he would be able

to take advantage of the fluid situation to improve his lot. At the outset he had to come to terms with the changes in everyday life that the new reality wrought. A housemaid was hired for a miniscule sum, and she came each morning from her home in the workers' quarter, leaving Ror's mother enough independence and free time to do whatever she desired. As a woman to whom life had clearly demonstrated that anything she did was to be for the betterment of her family, she decided to use her cleverness to serve them. Ror gave his mother intelligence assignments which she carried out with exactitude, like a good student working diligently at her homework.

Gradually, and with her characteristic thoroughness, Ror's mother explored the city in its every alleyway. She visited every place where access was allowed, taking in the bounty of gossip that leaked from around the tables of the aristocrats and those in positions of high command. Often she heard rumors that came through the filters of exaggeration and jealousy of those of average standing, but her sharp mind taught her to distinguish truth from falsehood. In the end the required information would be brought, partially filtered, to Ror's ears.

Ror and his mother quickly devised a system for analyzing the information, based on combining bits of data, and they came to be able to understanding and confirm information on any situation. Ror's family had been inclined to show a great political interest in what was happening around them, even while they were living in the workers' quarter. It was not clear from where this tendency had originated in a family that for all appearances was just like all the others. Perhaps it had been present in a previous generation and Ror's mother had a genetic predisposition to an intense political curiosity that she had passed down to Ror as well as to other family members.

One day, Ror's mother heard that by order of Queen Nefertiti an academy for the arts had opened. The main activity at the academy was to be the sculpting of the likeness of the queen, while sculpting of other royal personages would also be permitted. Nefertiti was known throughout the kingdom as the most beautiful woman in the world, and it was well known that King Akhenaton loved her with all his heart. The queen's beauty was mentioned in conversations, discussions, and gossip all over the country. The academy for the arts from time to time announced sculpting contests for which the main subject was the beauty of the queen. In this way the culture of the aristocracy was sometimes infiltrated by elements from the middle classes. This was a particular blessing since it afforded a suitable opening for the advancement of the arts, and was a promising method for identifying and encouraging talent. The academy put its reputation on the line when it initiated the sculpting contests, since it was also the critical and judging body. The contest dealt with two types of material: limestone and gypsum. Limestone was more difficult to work with, but it also held up better against damage. Gypsum was softer and easier to work with while less durable in hostile natural environments.

Ror's mother one day turned to her son and asked: "Why don't you try your hand at one of the contests?" Since he had no other satisfactory answer he decided that indeed he would give it a try.

Every one of the inhabitants of the city was very familiar with the facial features of Queen Nefertiti, since even in the old city, as now in the new, parades had taken place on occasion in which the queen presented all her radiant splendor to the loudly cheering people lining both sides of the road. Of course, in the old capitol it had not been possible to see the queen's face because of the crowds milling about, especially on the day of the great celebration that took place on the king's birthday. However here, in the newly built city, a smaller number of people positioned themselves on the sides of the route taken by the king's golden chariots where one could be intoxicated by the wondrous beauty of the divine queen. At this event there was always the expectation that the king might appear in the middle of the parade, and the procession would come to its joyous climax when Nefertiti, the beloved queen, joined the revered king. Ror and his family numbered among the merrymakers. Influenced by his mother, Ror had decided to sculpt the queen's likeness from memory. In actuality he had no choice since in those days citizens were not allowed to have in their possession a sketch or drawing of the queen that might bear imperfections, though it may have been a help to the artist. Ror's inroads into the art world helped him in his quest to understand the mysteries of the new religion that had become the way of life in the kingdom. It was a period in which many far-reaching changes were taking place in the different offices of the realm due the new divinity taking form.

An important facility for administrative control in the kingdom was the king's archive, which "Akhenaton" moved to the new capitol from the old one. The documents were made of mud slates written upon with sticks in the Accadian language, the international tongue of the world in that period. The "Amarna Archive" reveals that during the time when the capital of the country was Thebes, the pharaoh caused great difficulty for the governors of the various cities under his command, demanding payments of heavy taxes in the form of manpower, grain, meat, oil, and wine. The governors suffered under the burden of his rule and some even tried to revolt, but his resolute arm of the monarchy would press upon their napes until it had procured what the king wanted. Still and all, the period of the rule of "Akhenaton" was characterized by religious processions up and down the lengths of the city's main streets, and Ror and his family looked upon them and were impressed by their magnificence. Every time the religious procession marched down the street, it was preceded by an announcement that brought all the citizens outside to stand in front of their homes. The parade participants were the new religious priests dressed in colorful billowing garments, and as they passed by Ror's home the family members were ordered to bow to the priests with awe and respect. The event operated according to principles, which Ror had not yet grasped. To understand them would take some time in study - time that he and his family had not yet managed to eek out.

As "Akhetaton" developed and improved, so did Ror's personal status. He was placed in a senior position in the planning and construction of the capitol. The center of the city was designated to contain the royal palaces and temples that would serve also as administrative centers. Surrounding the central area, buildings were constructed in circular strips, one inside the other, getting larger the further they were from the center. These were the residential neighborhoods. Ror's family relocated yet again, to a new house in the closest strip to the center of town. Their new home had a spacious rectangular courtyard around which was a set of rooms was situated. Thutmose (who is Ror, as will be explained later) success extended also to the raising of his family. From his mother he inherited a sharp sense of how to succeed, and it would seem that his abilities were passed to his own offspring as well. Ror / Thutmose's first born son, Anen, was very fortunate in that King Akhenaton established himself in "Akhetaton" during the time of Ror's family's relocation from the workers' quarter to the center of the city. It so happened that the influence of the two – the king and Anen's father – grew in parallel, each within his own sphere, of course. His father's reputation within the halls of the palace paved the way for Anen within the appropriate offices, leading to his being assigned as minister of agriculture. Anen had inherited from his father both his talents and his loyalty to the regime, however unlike his father, he had no affinity for art or engineering. Instead, Anen proved himself to be an impressive manager of matters involving farming and taxes. His overseers valued his contributions and doors opened for Anen to make his way to the top.

Taxes were calculated according to the size of each farmer's holdings, so the power and wealth of the king depended upon the proper management of the country's land. The agricultural areas of Egypt extended along the length of the great river and the irrigation systems that were built surrounding it, in conjunction with the hot weather, made it possible to grow a wide variety of agricultural crops producing an abundance of food. However, because Egypt was almost completely devoid of rainfall, the fertility of the land of the Nile was mainly dependent on the yearly flooding of the river. Just as every Egyptian believed in the cycle of reincarnation, so the great river that provided the source of life had its own cycles. First came the flood followed by water's recession. The flood season spanned the months of June through September, bringing strong currents which carried sediments of red clay and many organic materials. This sediment, originating in the south of Egypt, was absorbed into the banks of the river, enriching the soil. When the flood ended, the season of sowing and watering arrived, lasting from October through February. Then came the harvesting of the crops from March through May, and after that began the season of high activity for Anen-son-of-Ror who was in charge of the collection of taxes.

As a result of Anen's success in agricultural matters, especially with regard to taxes, the government promoted him to a position requiring more complex skills. He was given the job of minister of the external empire. This job was particularly problematic since the rulers of the various neighboring states, those under the Egyptian control, battled among themselves in attempts to gain power and influence. Sometimes these governors were late in their payment of their taxes and Anen was forced once in a while, with the permission of his overseer, to send delegations of military troops to suppress any aggression by the leaders who had gone astray. The governor of Shechem, for example, was known as a habitual troublemaker. When he finally crossed a certain line of audacity, he was removed from his senior position and sent to the capitol to be put on trial. One night, while on the way to Egypt, the hapless governor escaped from the guards watching over his incarceration, but he was quickly caught and executed.

Unlike his older brother, who enjoyed political life, Thutmose's second son was drawn to the clergy. Since he came from a good home, he was accepted for studies opening up at the religious seminary that had been built near the temple, and the family had high expectations for him.

The family's prestige reached its peak when Thutmose won the competition for his bust of Queen Nefertiti. This happened after several years of trying to achieve the perfect creation. His father's long experience working with the rocks had been a help to Thutmose. From him he learned the skill of making a gradual transition between the hard limestone to the softer chalk. After experimenting with various materials he could work with to make these transitions, Thutmose decided upon the highest quality stone and from it he achieved the best bust of Nefertiti that it was possible to produce. However, even this result did not satisfy him. He finally decided to try to work in gypsum plaster, which he found worked best for forming the casing over the limestone sculpture.

As a result of all of his experimentation, Thutmose achieved a double-layer bust, the inner base of which was made of limestone while the outer layer was of plaster. On top of the plaster there appeared a third layer consisting of pigments used for the colors of the queen, including the hues of her orange complexion, her black eyes, the beads she wore around her neck, and her many-faceted royal head covering.

Thutmose made an appearance before the queen and presented to her the various busts he had made of her image. She examined them carefully, and to his great satisfaction she chose the bust that he liked the best. Queen Nefertiti raised her hand and pointing to the chosen sculpture she said: "This is the bust I want. What do you think?"

Thutmose bowed deeply and answered: "You have made a good choice Your Majesty. Were it up to me, that would be my preference as well."

The work later came to be known as "The famous bust of Nefertiti". Thutmose never explained to anyone the process he had used in his work. The combination of a layer of plaster over a base of lime he kept to himself as a trade secret. He expected that one day he would be asked to sculpt the likeness of Queen Nefertiti again, or that of some other royal personage.

Chapter Five:
The famous bust, a new religion, and beauty

Martin Klopstock, a doctoral student in archaeology working at a museum in Berlin, was very fortunate to be included as junior assistant to a delegation making the trip to Tel Amarna. The delegation would engage in the continuation of negotiations with the Egyptian authorities that were demanding the return of Queen Nefertiti's bust from Berlin to the place from which it had been taken. Martin Klopstock was brought along because of his erudite knowledge of sculpting materials and his familiarity with the ancient processes for work in limestone and gypsum plaster. The famous bust of Nefertiti had been discovered in proximity to a group of other statues from the time of the Pharaohs. The hope was that these sculptures, and others found over time, would prove to be authentic. There was always the fear that faked sculptures would cross the paths of the investigators. The head of the delegation from Berlin knew that his people were about to undergo a critical test of their findings. He hoped that the expertise of Martin Klopstock would assist in the matter of forgeries of the antiquities of the world, the Egyptian counterfeiters having a special reputation, even in the days of the Pharaohs.

When the famous bust of Nefertiti was discovered, there had not been a shred of doubt as to its authenticity.

When it was brought to Berlin, the question was raised as to how the name of the artist had been erased from this work, when it did appear on the bottom of other sculptures. Martin was among the researchers trying to understand the meaning of this discrepancy. At the time, it was not accepted practice for artists to sign their works, since all of their sculptures belonged to the monarchy. However, out of a desire to immortalize his name, Thutmose, like other artists, hid his signature in a way that made it possible to recognize only by using a reflecting tool on the bottom of the statue. This method of immortalization was discovered by Martin, thus adding an additional level of expertise to his credit. At that time, Martin's Jewish origins did not stand in his way, and he received the attention he deserved according to his contributions to society and not according to his ethnicity.

From the time that Martin discovered the signature of Thutmose on the statues of Nefertiti that had been created more than thirty-three hundred years earlier, he was profoundly affected by the brilliance of the famous bust and his heart was bound to its admired creator as if he had known him and had been influenced by his genius personally. Human history has documented other instances of mysterious connections creating psychological dependency between artists of the past and their admirers in the present. First, there was an obsessive connection on the part of the artist toward his work, and later there developed an obsession over the artist himself.

When the delegation returned from Egypt, Martin Klopstock finished his doctoral thesis, and a short time later he was appointed curator of the images of Queen Nefertiti. The name Nefertiti means, "the beautiful woman has arrived". Her image was as unique and enticing as her name, and left a deep impression on Martin. The task fell to Dr. Klopstock to gather information about the character of this queen, thought to be the most beautiful of all by the entire enlightened world. There naturally arises a dilemma with regard to this, since there was no lack of women in the world who would assign to themselves, or were assigned by others, this same distinction.

The beautiful Helen of Troy was one of these. She was the wife of the Greek Menelaus, and was known as the most beautiful of all women. When she was kidnapped by Paris and brought to Troy, the Greek navy went out to surround Troy bringing about an extended war that resulted in much bloodshed. This is why Helen of Troy became known as having "the face that launched a thousand ships".

Nefertiti lived approximately one hundred years before Helen. The special bust of the Egyptian queen having come into the hands of the Germans gave Nefertiti the advantage, and justified in the eyes of Dr. Klopstock his ignoring Helen and focusing instead on the uniqueness of Nefertiti's beauty.

And there was something else that forged the soul connection between Martin and the image of Nefertiti.

Martin's occupation with her bust started a short time after he married his heart's desire, his love, Clara, whom he had met at the university. It had been love at first sight, as in the movies, a love that lit up his spirit.

Clara's high-heeled shoes looked like natural extensions of her legs. She had a regal walk, poised and steady without making any effort, and her elegant clothes fit her perfectly naturally. She preferred tailored two-piece suits over skirts and blouses, and on cold days she was likely to her to cover her hands with gloves in a color perfectly matched to her shoes. More than anything, Martin loved her golden hair, caught up at her nape in a long ponytail, accentuating her long neck.

Martin was not the only man who admired the young art student's beauty. He had to stand his ground for Clara's heart against students from the department of archeology, and even against young men who came from the schools of engineering and medicine to court her. But, Martin had no real competition. He was able to offer her an especially worthy feeling. With him, she felt like a princess meeting a many-virtued man who stood above the others in his intelligence and his devotion.

The seriousness and aspiration to perfection with which Martin approached every subject he put his mind to were what ensured his successes in life.

Clara had her heart's desirev – to see herself as a woman from whom nothing is demanded from her connection with an admired perfectionist. In his eyes, she knew, she was considered the one and only, and the most beautiful in the world. Perhaps this is the reason she was so hurt by the disappointing setback when she found out that Martin's devotion to his work was transporting him away from her and into different world. Even though it was a virtual existence with no basis in reality, his love and devotion to the mythical Nefertiti made Clara feel extremely jealous, and she felt the disgrace of a woman betrayed.

Martin wasn't sure if it was coincidence or the hand of god that brought about the outward resemblance between the two women. At first he thought his imagination was playing tricks on him and he began to wonder if perhaps he was suffering from some kind of perversion. There was a period of time when he would test himself daily to be sure that the resemblance actually existed and that his love for Clara had not somehow clouded his judgment. In the end Martin decided to invite Clara to participate in these deliberations. Clara was very pleased to hear of the vexing dilemma her husband was dealing with. Was she so very beautiful that she even resembled the ancient queen of Egypt, the one that everyone was talking about without end in the halls of the university?

One day she said emphatically: "Take me to her."

The meeting of the two women greatly excited Clara, and she came home feeling quite proud of herself. "Martin my dear, you were not wrong at all. There is definitely a significant likeness between the two of us, " she said, her face glowing with pride.

Martin was pleased with the validation he received from Clara about the beauty of the bust. His wife's support encouraged him to invest even more effort in his work. He did not yet sense the psychological difficulties that befall a man carrying the burden of two great loves.

Unwittingly, Dr. Klopstock was caught in the eternal question: Are preferences for beauty created by human cultures in a process that differs from place to place and from time to time? Or is perhaps the human being born with particular tendencies to prefer beauty, independent of geography? When Martin's research across generations revealed Nefertiti's unwavering place at the top of the scale of feminine beauty, he came to the conclusion that the appreciation of beauty is not dependent on time or place. In the infant's brain there already exists a framework for recognition of beauty from the moment of birth.

In addition to Dr. Klopstock's special devotion to the bust of Nefertiti, he had a particular interest in Amenhotep IV who while married to Nefertiti had brought about a religious revolution in Egypt, centered around one supreme god. That intersection of the first monotheistic religion - which interested him as a Jew - and the most beautiful woman in the world, captured the scientific imagination and rocked the emotional life of Dr. Klopstock. According to writings preserved from the beginning of Dr. Klopstock's employ at the museum, he was also fascinated with the number 18. Amenthotep IV belonged to the 18th dynasty, and the "eighteen" is a prayer central to the Jewish weekday worship that is recited in the morning, afternoon, and evening.

Martin gathered every single detail possible, and was well on top of everything that was known about the lives of the king and his wife. And they became the center of his own life.

Certain aspects of the mummification process undergone by Amenhotep III after his death were also of interest to Martin, as a Jew. In his notes, Martin showed his strong, perhaps unconscious, identification with the process of the soul's transmigration after death, in spite of that concept not being accepted by believers in the Jewish religion. He was familiar with the journey of estrangement taken by the Jews of the Diaspora as they wandered from land to land, country to country, for thousands of years. Often the thought of the wandering of the Jews in this world reminded him of the Egyptian transmigration of the soul when it departed from it.

Martin placed particular attention on the ideological aspects involved in death and resurrection according to the Egyptian perception. In addition to the condition of the body, the soul's return to life depended upon the results of a trial of "objective truth". [The heart of the deceased was weighed on a scale at this trial], since according to Egyptian religion, the weight of the heart was the deciding factor when considering the fate of the soul of the deceased. If the person's deeds during his time in this world were deemed worthy [his heart was neither too light nor too heavy], he would achieve life after death.

The Pharaohs had built temples all over ancient Egypt in honor of Amon and the rest of the gods of that old religion, including the famous temple at Karnak. Amenhotep IV took over the kingdom after his father's thirty-eight year reign. In the fifth year of his own kingship he officially changed his name to Akhenaton (meaning "worthy of serving Aton). In the seventh year, the capitol city was relocated to Akhetaton in the western wilderness, and the construction of the city went on for two more years.

In the ninth year of his reign, Akhenaton declared Aton to be the only god permitted to worship, and ordered the destruction of all the temples of other gods in Egypt. This dealt a fatal blow to the priests, the clergy of Amon, who until that day had wielded great political and economic power in Egypt.

The religion of Aton forbade the creation of idols or statues of the god, except for the form of a sun-disk with rays of light radiating fanlike from the face in the shape of hands representing the unseen spirit of Aton that creates all life in the universe.

One of the most amazing figures of that time, a person whose life began as part of the working class and who at his peak achieved almost completely free access to the palace of the king, was the artist Thutmose. At birth his parents gave him the name Ror, but upon his rise to greatness after the discovery of his talents in the limestone quarries, he exchanged it for Thutmose, after the great warrior King Thutmose III. King Thutmose III conquered and annexed to Egypt the lands surrounding the kingdom, and he was victorious in the famous battle of Megiddo in the land of Canaan. Dr. Martin Klopstock learned of all this while researching the prominent artist's history. Among all of Thutmose's praiseworthy attributes, Martin was able to discern the romantic soul hidden within his hero.

In time, when he had become the artist of the court of King Akhenaton, Thutmose became privy to discussions of the fascinating goings-on that originated in the palace, often accompanied by jealousy and hatred that expanded and infiltrated beyond the walls that surrounded them. While the artist gave some attention to the whisperings about the virtues and the shortcomings of his patron the king, his main interest was Queen Nefertiti, whose beauty continued to mesmerize him.

At first Thutmose had great admiration for the king. However, once accustomed to royal life he came to have some doubts and questions. What had motivated him to abandon with such urgency the old capitol that had served the Pharaohs before him, and to relocate in a new place? What caused him to change the Egyptian religion into something completely different?

Thutmose had been taught since childhood to worship the god Ra. It was difficult for him to transfer his feelings and allegiance to the king's new god. Ra was god of the sun, and he followed the path of the sun each day from east to west. Then, from sunset until sunrise the next day, the sun god continued in a boat, through the netherworld underneath the surface of earth. He could complete his journey only as long as he was not attacked along the way by the giant serpent monster, Apophis. This was the doctrine taught to Ror from as early as he could remember.

The king was not satisfied with Ra the sun god. He wanted Aton to be the sun itself. Akhenaton took advantage of the fact that the god Ra had lost some of his prestige in the eyes of the Egyptians who had begun to prefer another sun god – Horus. He decreed that Aton was not only the supreme god, but that he was the only god, the universal god in the shape of the sun disk outstretching its hands as rays of light toward the earth, to protect the faithful. The new religious doctrine held that Akhenaton was the only one who could intervene between Aton and his people.

Much vacillation and vicissitude of thought plagued Thutmose's spirit until he began to ask himself: If everything revolves exclusively around the sun, as the present king claims, does this not involve an essential contradiction? From the time when the first Pharaoh sat on his golden throne, was not the sun supposed to protect the house of the monarchy and the inhabitants of Egypt, and to serve the leaders living on the soil of the earth, such as the great river served them?! This being so, clearly the sun rotates around the earth and is not the center of the universe. However, Thutmose knew his place, and he understood that legitimate changes took place in religion over the span of generations. After all, in the city of Thebes when the sun-god Ra and the god Amon had been unified into the god "Amon-Ra", this was accepted with great respect. And too, he knew that even this unified god was about to fall from glory, since the time had come for the new god, Aton.

Thutmose heard rumblings and rumors saying that the changes the king was making in the kingdom stemmed from the influence of his wife, Nefertiti. After all, she came from Mitanni, the land where strange religious ideas were born. Thutmose did not believe the rumors, since as far as he knew Nefertiti's interest in religious precepts was minimal. Those who hated the queen circulated the story that Nefertiti had tried, and perhaps succeeded, to take advantage of Thutmose in order get back at her husband who had abandoned her in favor of Queen Kiya, the other wife who had "invaded" the palace and assumed her place in the king's bed. The story was passed around because of the people's desire to "know the truth."

This rumor was in direct contradiction to the wonderful pictures found that emphasized the harmony between the king and his queen, Nefertiti, though it's possible these depicted the time before the start of the emotional distance between the two. Dr. Martin Klopstock pored over the documents of El Amarna in which he discovered the period of time in which was described the behavior of the royal Egyptian rulers. Martin noticed that changes in the behaviors of the residents of the palace did not always fit the calendar of the king's archive.

As a young man, Martin appreciated the tenderness and femininity of his wife, Clara, however had not enough experience with women to understand the ups and downs of her spirit. He had not yet become sensitive enough to notice the changes in his relationship with his wife with respect to his emotional ties to the subject of his research, his beloved Nefertiti. Clara was quickly becoming extremely upset by the perceived competition. One evening, unexpectedly, she told him in a tone of reprimand: "Martin my dear, don't you think it oversteps the boundaries of good taste for you to keep regaling me with stories of the wonderful Nefertiti?" This was said after Clara and her husband had lain down in their bed and poured themselves the choice semi-sweet Kaiser Stuhl wine produced in the Rhine Valley. He wore the pajamas she had pressed for him, and over her body skimmed a partly transparent nightgown. She was surprised when he chose that moment to tell her about new discoveries he had made that morning, discoveries having to do with the raw materials used to sculpt the revered bust of the beautiful Nefertiti.

Her question stopped him cold. He didn't answer, which was his second mistake, since the annoyed Clara interpreted his silence as disregard for what she had asked.

It turned into a decidedly unsatisfactory evening. Instead of experiencing a lovely partaking of wine that would lead to a sensory experience they would both enjoy, they turned out the lights amidst an unpleasant argument. Though they did not intend it, there followed a series of disagreements that caused turbulence in their relationship, and at the center of it all stood the question of Nefertiti's place in the life of the couple.

"I'm sorry Clara. Until now you always enjoyed hearing about the new developments with regard to Nefertiti. You rejoiced in the advancement of my research. What suddenly happened to change that?"

She did not answer. His question only inflamed her anger. He doesn't understand me at all, she thought to herself. It's true, at first I did join in his happiness over his successes, but he doesn't understand that there have to be limits to these things. He showed me the resemblance between us but is that enough reason for him to put all of his attention on her at my expense? Clara remained quiet.

"Your silence means you are angry at me. I don't understand you. Have you been told that I am having an affair with another woman? Perhaps a student at the university? Nefertiti lived more than three thousand years ago", he said, trying to calm her.

Martin did not understand that his explanation yielded results exactly opposite of what he had intended. His words only expanded Clara's frustration. She realized that she did not have the ways and means to get back to her singular standing where he was hers alone. Although Clara was Martin's wife, the recognition for his scientific abilities and the prizes he hoped to win in the future, all rested upon her opponent.

She finally answered, "I have concluded that when there is a conflict between a man and a woman caused by the inappropriate behavior of the man, and he does not understand his culpability, then no explanation will be helpful until he recognizes his mistakes himself."

Martin felt wounded, "And what do you find me guilty of? Have I done some wrong deed? Have I betrayed you?"

She wanted to answer, "yes, you betrayed me with your thoughts", but the words did not pass her lips. She hesitated to say such a thing since it sounded tasteless, even though it was completely true. How could have an affair with a woman who is no longer alive?

In addition to his occupation with the sculptures of Nefertiti, the artist was expected to satisfy other desires of the king. Thutmose wondered about the Akenaton's appearance in the works of art being created to immortalize him. The King preferred that his image be depicted with bodily deformities – such as an elongated head, skinny hands and feet, the wide hips of a female, and a protruding belly. Whatever for? To his amazement, Thutmose discovered that other members of the royal family also been depicted having protruding bellies, wide hips, and thin hands and feet.

Thutmose did not have the scientific understanding that would allow him to examine the significance of these deformities in the king's family. He tried to figure out their meaning. Did they hold some kind of spiritual meaning that the king was trying to convey? Did the king expect his body to change of the course of his life? Or perhaps his body really was quite different from the average build in ways that would be difficult to conceal? When the king was asked to assume certain positions to facilitate the artist's work on the sculpture, he did not comply, but rather demanded that Thutmose carry out his demands.

When Thutmose met with Nefertiti and asked her for an explanation of her husband's strange behavior, he got frank response which surprised him greatly. "Have you considered all the possible results from the combining of seed within the royal family?"

Even more surprised than Thutmose had been, was Martin Klopstock as he examined the material from three thousand years earlier. Had Nefertiti understood that marriage within families had a negative impact on the quality of the royal race? Martin mulled over the question as to whether the royal family suffered from a genetic defect. And more importantly, was Nefertiti's behavior toward her husband influenced by his physical deformities and her strange thought about their meaning? If so, to what extent?

One day, Nefertiti said to the king, "Perhaps you'll take me for a tour of the kingdom? We can said the length of the great river. I am told that during this season of the year the river is teaming with sailing vessels large and small, with sails of every color. Instead of the irritating sunshine we have here, we will enjoy the nice light breeze. We can alight from time to time on the shore and the citizens will greet us with respect and shower us with love. I so enjoy the sight of crowds of workers and slaves prostrated on the ground and bowing politely in our honor. You can show them what a beautiful wife you have."

Akhenaton regarded her with a mixture of love and astonishment and answered, "My dear, your beauty surpassed that of all that is mine in the kingdom". Nothing would make me happier than a pleasant vacation with you on the river. We would have music and singing and dancing on the boat, and we would lack for nothing. But I have many responsibilities here, during the construction of the new city. I want to make sure that my people build the castle and the temple as they should, and as quickly as required. If I were to myself away on a pleasure trip it would be misunderstood, I am sorry my dear."

A solution was presently found to the problem. Nefertiti went on her trip on the royal boat on the great river, alone, in the name of the king. After the first very successful voyage, additional very interesting trips were arranged. The nation adored the queen who on her various dispatches took pains to visit them in town centers as well as remote places, taking an interest in their activities and their difficulties.

"I am receiving very good reports about your river journeys," said the king on day. "These trips are improving the reputation of the royal monarchy," he added.

Nefertiti tried to take in his words of praise expressing honest satisfaction, thinking that may be hiding feelings of jealousy. She felt a certain change in his tone. At first he expressed true words of pure praise, but as time passed there were more and more signs of a concealed bitterness. She tried several times to repeat her request that he join her in the sailings, but he responsibilities surrounding the new religion kept growing with time.

Nefertiti came to understand that her husband was more comfortable on solid ground, where everything remains where it belongs, with no change. What he set down at night in a certain place must be found there the next morning. He preferred routine with no surprises to the ups and downs of the waves of the river, appearing out of nowhere and then disappearing, wandering every day, every hour, and every moment from one place to another.

Nefertiti knew how to entertain herself during her time of being engrossed in her travels on the river, all to herself, surrounded by adoring servants and attendants ready to respond to her every utterance and to satisfy every whim that came to her mind. Each evening the best musicians played for her the songs of her country that she loved to hear. For her pleasure they played upon flutes, harps, trumpets, bells, cymbals, trombones, and drums.

One night, attractive female dancers with taught bodies made a presentation of their talents as well as their skills in the seduction of men, but this performance only proved to the queen that she had nothing to learn in that arena.

While Nefertiti took in all of the best and most beautiful that her entertainers presented to her on the boat, it was her habit to sip the finest nectars that the kingdom could offer. Her preference was for the "blue lotus nymphaea", which contained psychoactive matter which had a narcotic effect and caused its users to hallucinate.

Queen Nefertiti liked to play a game called senet, well known and popular game among the ancient aristocracy. In Egyptian culture many aspects of life were tied to religion, and it was believed that one who knew how to play senet was under the protection of the gods. Senet was a board game played on a table-top, in a similar manner to chess. According to an ancient drawing of Queen Nefertiti, the pieces were moved around the board using a stick having one wide and one narrow end, resembling a very small cricket bat. The captain of the vessel knew that each evening when playing with the Queen he must respectfully concede.

Before one of the queen's expeditions on the great river she had an idea. She brought Thutmose on board and asked him to continue to work on his sculpture. The queen soon noticed that Thutmose's art improved when he worked on the boat. During their time on the river he tried a new and different styles of sculpting her likeness. On the boat he lacked certain materials and conditions afforded by his studio, but the building of an art room containing all the most important items lessoned this problem.

Akhenaton's earliest intimate relations with women other than Nefretiti saddened Dr. Martin Klopstock because of his deeply felt connection with the queen. Information from the writings of El Amarna documented the fact that Tiye, Akhenaton's mother, continued to rule for an extended period after the death of his father during the time running parallel to when Akhenaton was already ruling as king of Egypt. This meant that he and his mother ruled Egypt together as man and wife. As such, the two set an example of incest. This did not jive with information Martin read about the adversarial relationship between them at the outset of Akhenaton's rule, but it is possible that the needs of state obligated them to come to reconciliation. It is also not understood how such a relationship could have occurred in the face of the great love between Akhenaton and his wife Nefertiti in the early years of his reign.

Akhenaton's preference for his second wife, Kiya, at the expense of Nefertiti his official royal wife, also bothered Martin. And an additional complication was added when toward the end of the period of his rule, Akhenaton took Ankhesenpaaten, his third daughter, to be his last wife. Martin was engrossed for quite a while in his studies of these complicated relations between the sexes among the royals, yet he never completely understood them.

Directly following the death of Akhenaton, the

religion of Aton that he had headed stopped functioning. Tutankh rose to the throne as an eight year old child, and changed his name to Tutankhamun. In the third year of his kingship (1348 to 1331 BCE) Tutankhamun abandoned Akhetaton, and the city turned to rubble. The palaces and temples built by Akhenaton, including the shrine at Neve Amon, were neglected and destroyed in the time of his heirs, who turned them into sources of building materials for the construction and decoration of their shrines. Inscriptions that had been dedicated to Aton were destroyed and erased, and the name of the revolutionary king were stricken from the history of the Pharaohs, and did not appear in any of the references made by the later kings. The priests of Amon, it appeared, destroyed everything in the heat of anger at the religion of Aton. "This raging anger between the leaders of different religions has not changed significantly between that time and the present", wrote Martin in his notebook.

The surviving remnants of Akhenaton's time as Pharaoh were finally brought to light when scientists discovered them at the end of the nineteenth century. Martin was one of the archeologists who gathered the relics of Akhenaton's kingdom, and many broken pieces of holy vessels passed through his hands – object that had served with full splendor in the temples of the kingdom passed through his hands. He was reminded of an attempt that had been made during his own lifetime to erase from the pages of history a great and prominent culture.

On May 10, 1933, an infamous ceremony of festive book-burning took place in Berlin's Opera Square, initiated by Germany's Propaganda Minister. About twenty thousand volumes by two hundred writers were set aflame. These authors were scientists, philosophers, artists, and journalists who were Jews, communists, and liberals against the regime. The books were plundered from many libraries and private collections. Among the books that were burned were works by Thomas Mann and his brother Heinrich Mann, Heinrich Heine, Karl Marx, Sigmund Freud, Erich Kastner, and many others.

A monument commemorating these contemptible deeds was erected in the Bebelplatz on March 20, 1995. The elderly Dr. Martin Klopstock intended to be present for the ceremony but his waning strength did not allow it. He passed away several days beforehand. His wife Clara had died three years earlier. Their son Carl and his family, having come from Israel, were at his bedside at the moment of his death.

Chapter Six:
Dangerous Love and the
Curse of the Pharaohs

It was not clear to Martin at what point the artist-subject relationship between Thutmose and Nefertiti changed into an intimate love affair. This was a very dangerous development, since it would be hard to imagine that Akhenaton, whom Thutmose so admired, and to whom he owed an enormous debt of gratitude for having raised his status to that of an aristocratic member of the king's court, and who had made possible the conditions that allowed him to reach the peak expression of his artistic talent, would be pleased to discover intimate relations taking place between his loyal subject and his wife. Clearly, the king had the ability to destroy the artist all at once should he find out about the betrayal.

When Martin first discovered the relationship (which was so intense it put to shame the sun and the moon), his admiration for Thutmose was enhanced. The affair seemed to show that great courage numbered among the positive qualities of the great sculptor.

"How is the work coming along?" asked Nefertiti of Thutmose one day.

"Not badly, I think", he answered.

"I am anxious to see", she told him.

"I ask of you, my queen, just a drop more patience."

"But you know I am not patient," she answered and flashed him her charming smile. "I never have been, and I never will be."

Thutmose was very familiar with the inviting smile that was unique to the queen. He stood up from his gold plated chair, went to her and knelt. Her head was bent toward him, and taking it into both his hands, he planted a protracted kiss on her painted lips.

"One more," he heard her say.

He fulfilled that request and added, "I think that in four weeks time I shall have a product I can show you."

"Perhaps it will be less than four weeks?"

"Perhaps, but it's hard for me to promise."

"Do you think I'll be beautiful?"

"The most beautiful in the world," he answered.

"Pity that you are not my man always," she told him.

"We must separate dream from reality," he responded.

"How unfortunate that you are right," she agreed, "I am happy that my husband gave you this job."

"It was not only he. It was you as well."

"How will my nose be?" came the question.

"I have tried make it straight, and so it shall be" he answered.

"Good." Queen Nefertiti regarded the brilliant bust that stood before her and continued with her inquiry. "And the lips?"

You will have pretty lips, a little bit sensitive, but not too much so," he answered her.

"Why not? I quite prefer fleshy lips," said Nefertiti.

"I don't think you should go too far. It would look artificial and people might form a negative opinion about you and about me."

"What about the neck?"

"You will have a divine neck, as long as I can possibly make it without exceeding the boundaries of good taste."

"Excellent. And the chest?"

"Well, we agreed that I should sculpt only the upper chest, to accentuate your long neck", he told her.

"What? Do I not have attractive enough breasts?"

"I do not say that - remember, that is what you have claimed."

"Ha! Alright, we'll leave it as it is," she said.

"Large breasts like those of a dancer in a tavern are not befitting a queen," he said.

"Perhaps you are right," agreed Nefertiti, secretly pleased with his comment.

"You know, they are already talking about us," he told her. Gossip about the special relations between the two had found its way into the corridors of the palace and the temple as well.

"Let them talk," she responded.

"You once told me it would not be good for us," he said.

"Do you want us to stop meeting?" she asked him.

"We must meet, at least until we complete the bust," he answered with a decisiveness that pleased her.

"Then continue!" she said assertively, "Meanwhile I will discuss it with my husband."

He was alarmed. "What will you discuss with him?"

"I will attempt to convince him that he should not believe the evil gossip", she explained.

"And if you do not succeed in convincing him?" came the question.

"I will succeed," she answered. "And besides, he is now very busy with his Kiya". The smile disappeared from her face. "I have no idea what he sees in her."

Thutmose was starting to hear rumblings about a conflict between Nefertiti and the other wife. The story that was caught and tossed about in the wheels of gossip rolling through the palace was that the royal seamstress who had served Nefertiti loyally for a long time was pressed into service to the new queen, Kiya, as well. Nefertiti, who knew how to turn any new situation to her advantage, secretly ordered her faithful seamstress to "make mistakes" in her sewing of Kiya's dresses such that they would bring out her unattractive features and hide her beauty. To achieve her objective she convinced the seamstress that the new queen had an asymmetric figure – one that was a match to the twisted body of the king. Since the royal seamstress was given to understand that Kiya's body was not worthy of high quality tailoring, the result was to Nefertiti's adversary's detriment. However, soon Kiya began to have suspicions, and she hired a professional seamstress of her own whose income would be dependent upon the satisfaction of her employer.

Thutmose was upset by this rumor, the details of

which did not surprise him since he well knew the queen's tendencies.

Thutmose also heard that there was a pact of silence between the king and queen, the purpose of which was to prevent scandals that could result from the love affairs that Akhenaton and Nefertiti engaged in outside of their marriage, and damage both their reputations. Akhenaton, as the son of God, had problems with image. He wanted to be seen as an enlightened ruler, preserving the sanctity of the family line and making sure that nothing external contaminated its purity. Some news he received from the royal physician furthered this goal. The doctor found Nefertiti to have transitioned early into the phase of life where there was no chance at all of her being fertile any longer. Knowing this, Thutmose, thinking logically, found it reasonable that Nefertiti could ward off a scandal by talking to the king sensibly and that she would get what she wanted, as always. He didn't like to admit it, but as his special relationship with Nefertiti took hold, jealousy had taken hold in his heart. He had feelings that wavered between envy and animosity toward the king, who despite his many shortcomings, physical and otherwise, had Nefertiti always as his own, for as long as he should desire her.

Thutmose hesitated to inquire about the king's bodily deformity because of the sensitivity of the subject, yet the subject often bothered him, especially when he was sitting in front of him and receiving his instructions. The total intimacy the lovers experienced allowed a level of openness such, so he thought, that even if he was not given the complete answer he was striving for, his place at Nefertiti's side was enough assured that a question of this sort would not distance him from her. So he believed, and as it turned out he was not mistaken.

When Thutmose posed the question as to whether the king's body was actually distorted, his clothing concealing the fact from view, the queen responded, "Why do you think I'm in love with you?"

Nefertiti was seen as a strong woman in the eyes of those who were gossiping about her disgrace. The stories about her manipulative tendencies circulated all the hours of the day and night among the kingdom's subjects. Everyone saw her as an enterprising personality who was very sure of herself. Nefertiti did not try to refute the gossip. "Let them think that's what I'm like!" she said to herself. The only person who sensed her fragility was Thutmose, and later it was understood by Martin as well. From time to time she had her doubts about whether Thutmose really loved her as he would have her believe. These concerns were accompanied by the constant fear that he may be taking advantage of her, using her as a ladder on which to climb to a higher rank at the palace. But this uncertainty about his loyalty would disappear when she saw the great devotion with which he worked on her statue and his efforts to ensure her depiction was as beautiful as it could be.

The two people closest to her possessed attributes that were quite opposite from one another. In Thutmose she found a combination of powerful masculinity and great physical strength. This combination made magic happen when paired with his active and fertile imagination. He could turn an inanimate shapeless slab of stone into a divine and captivating figure that looked upon those who saw it and determined their earthly fates. In contrast, her omnipotent husband had physical drawbacks. There was especially room for improvement in his performance in bed. He had the body of a deformed youth, supported by very thin legs, and he tried to conceal his emaciated arms under his garments. However, these defects did not lesson the admiration he received. He had manifestations of masculinity that she had a difficulty understanding. He was endowed a toughness that was beyond reproach. Akhenaton set himself the goal of building a new capitol city and to create a new divine religion, and was not deterred by any of the dangers that stood in his way. This combination of vision and decisiveness made him fit for the kingship, in spite of his defects. Of this she was certain.

Thutmose had drawn extremely close to the woman he desired, he was very successful in his work and his art, and he received professional recognition among other artists, yet inside he suffered from deep frustration that cut to his very flesh. The nation bestowed on him much praise, but the highest accolade of all, the "King's Prize", he had yet to receive. When once in a while he was asked by his colleagues why this recognition had been denied him, he would answer modestly, with a forced air of acceptance, that the honor and respect they had already afforded him was more than enough, and he required nothing more.

After an intoxicating carnal meeting on the day she celebrated her arrival in this world, under the mocking crescent moon that knew all of his secrets, Thutmose tried to make use of the electricity their bodies created and Nefertiti's excitement by saying "Is there any truth to what everyone thinks - that the king values my work?" he exhaled the question from his lungs.

"Why do you ask this?" came the response.

"I suspect that he does not support the work we are doing together," answered Thutmose.

She turned her head to face him, the gesture implying a question to which he answered, "Would you find out from him why I do not have his favor?"

She must have understood very well his intention that inviting evening. At that moment, she wanted his body, but did not need his soul, and had even less use for his smooth talk. She did not answer him - either because she did not know the answer, or because she chose not to know. "If you know what's good for you, I will do the asking," she finally whispered.

And he knew.

Thutmose never knew, however, whether Nefertiti made any actual efforts with the king on his behalf. The fact that he never did win the "King's Prize" in his lifetime, caused him to carry a great burden of suffering and disappointment. When the great artist disappeared from the palace and its environs, rumors made their rounds in the homes of the aristocracy about mysterious connections between his not receiving the prize, his disappearance, and his intimate relationships.

Martin's feelings about Thutmose were mixed. He admired him and wanted to see him as perfect, and as superior to other mortals. As a scientist, Martin knew the taboos that were at play. Judgment should be made only according to the rules of truth. But as a personality having been overcome by an historic figure who seemed to him larger than life, Martin sometimes could not stay within the norms, and when he uncovered the merits and shortcomings of Nefertiti, there slowly crept into his heart the fear that when Thutmose made his works of art depicting Nefertiti, he had not always succeeded in objectivity when it came to her charms, and had tended to see, hear and feel things, even if they were seemingly beyond the boundaries of the reality in which he worked.

It was not very difficult for Martin to reconstruct the conversations that might have taken place between the queen and her new lover. He wrote them in the notebook that was always with him at work. This was a research notebook that was intended to contain only proven facts gathered by using the scientific method. However Martin, like some other scientists, sometimes blended proven facts with ideas that were imagined or thought up as a result of his research.

"Finally, I am loved by a real man," he heard her say.

"If you wish it, this can continue until His Majesty catches us and has my head cut off," Thutmose whispered his answer.

"I am certain that a man such as yourself can continue to perform even after the king removes your head," she came back with sudden laughter.

Thutmose felt his heart constrict when he heard her words and decided not to offer a response.

"I am sorry, my love, about what I said. It only demonstrates how much I admire your abilities," Nefertiti whispered to him, as she licked his cheek and his ear.

"For you this is a joke. For me it could mean the end of my sojourn in this world", he answered.

"Please accept my apology. Apparently I am really as cruel as the gossips report me to be," she said, and her hand slid slowly toward his genitals as she prepared to join their bodies for another emotional discharge.

"Come let me do that which you like me to do, and don't think for a moment that I am not in the same danger as you."

When they finished, she whispered again, "There is not, and there never was, another man like you."

Looking over what he had written in his notebook about their lovemaking, Martin asked himself if perhaps the last sentence uttered by the queen was a bit of an exaggeration. That last utterance may have been influenced too much by the concealed feelings of admiration in his own heart toward Thutmose. Martin took great pains to collect all the information available about the life of Thutmose, since for him the sculptor of the bust of Nefertiti was not a mythical character, but an actual and respected work partner who occupied his thoughts day and night. What most preoccupied him was the question of the physical relations between Thutmose and Nefertiti and the love they felt for one another. Were these only the result of Nefertiti's feeling of being abandoned by Akhenaton when Queen Kiya started to share his bed?

Martin slowly began to feel the heavy burden of his hidden emotions. His adoration of Thutmose was gradually giving way to a troubled feeling about the man he had been so accustomed to admiring. Could he really be jealous of a man who had captured a woman's heart thousands of years ago? His hopeless avarice could never see the light of day, yet Martin maintained that it was not completely without meaning! He had begun his work on Nefertiti with clear logical thinking, and only during the protracted research process had he become fettered by his tremulous emotions surrounding his subject, and had unwittingly become entwined in what he feared was a foolish, yet uncontrollable, love. Was not what Martin felt when he stumbled and was caught in the net of Nefertiti similar to the meek desire Samson had for Delilah?

During the period preceding the outbreak of World War II, in moments when Martin's thoughts were caught up in the subject of Nefertiti, Clara's day-to-day presence served to loosen his obsession with his research on the bust of the ancient queen. The resemblance between the two created an emotional sublimation. This happened after one of his arguments with Clara had ended in a standoff and he understood that his wife's complaints toward him had some merit. From that time on, he tried to refrain from mentioning Nefertiti in the presence of Clara. Clara knew that his retreat was only partial. She was well aware that it would be quite impossible for him to banish the queen completely from his thoughts.

The couple fell into a routine whereby they were happy only to a certain extent. Martin and Clara tried to become as close to one another as they could manage, but they struggled with the barrier between them that was Nefertiti.

On the days that Clara awoke in good spirits she started her day with the connection between the sun and moon echoing in her mind. On such days, she, Clara, was the sun, and Nefertiti was in her own orbit, far from the sun. But on gloomy mornings the picture changed, and Nefertiti turned into the sun while she, Clara, was the lusterless moon.

During the war, new conditions came into being causing Martin to be separated against his will from his family, and their continued survival was in question. He fought for his daily existence, on his own, and then everything changed. He missed Clara intensely and he took advantage of every opportunity he had to express how he felt about her, in his waking moments and in his dreams. Sometimes Clara would be interchanged with Nefertiti, but these visions were always short-lived. The less complicated and more stable relationship was the one between Nefertiti and Thutmose. Thinking about that couple did not put his marriage in danger. It tugged at his heart, but in a way that he could endure.

Martin was gifted with an enormous strength of will, as was demonstrated by his surviving the war. While he succeeded at getting over his mixed feelings with respect to the warm relations between Thutmose and his queen, and his feelings surrounding this had cooled off, he still had difficulties understanding the nature of the personal relations within the palace. Martin tried insofar as was possible, to dig into the complexity of relationships in the royal house and to become like "one of the family", but he succeeded only in part. While marital relationships among the masses were modest and took place within the accepted framework of monogamy, the situation among the royals was far from simple, and in fact sometimes was unimaginably complex. Ankhesenamun, the third daughter of Akhenaton and Nefertiti, married her father when she was twelve years old, and together they produced a daughter. After her father's death, Ankhesenamun married Tutankhamun and became Queen of Egypt. They had two children who died at birth. During the ninth year of his reign, at the age of eighteen, Tutankhamun suddenly died. At the time of his death Ankhesenamun was twenty-one years old. She married Ay in order for him to become Pharaoh, according to the rules of the monarchy. Ankhesenamun passed to the next world in the year 1322 before the common era. This complicated chain of events prevented Dr. Martin Klopstock from being able to figure out exactly at what times each of his heroes played their parts in the Pharaoh's house, nor could he get a clear picture of the conditions under which Nefertiti and Thutmose met – both for the purpose of the sculpting of the famous bust, and to consummate their love.

Marriage within the royal family was subject to many changes over the course of the period of the Egyptian Pharaohs. Much importance was placed upon the rank of the king's wife, especially with respect to the conventions of hierarchy during when the king chose to deviate from monogamy, into polygamy. The highest title a woman could receive was that of "Great Royal Wife". Less important than she were the "secondary wives", and concubines were not counted within the hierarchy. Marriage within the family created more complications. During the time of Amenhotep III and his son Akhenaton the perception was held that intra-family marriage would preserve the purity of the lineage and prevent contamination of the royal bloodline. As a result of this belief, kings would couple with their sisters, half sisters, or other female family members. In most cases, the woman did not have the right to object to the marriage, and the agreement was made her father and the groom. The Great Royal Wife held an especially important position, since in order to ensure the continuation of the royal family, every would-bc Pharaoh was required to take a wife. As the preeminent woman of the kingdom, the Great Royal Wife stood beside her husband at all official rites and ceremonies. Also of significance was the custom by which the heir to the throne would marry the eldest daughter of the Great Royal Wife, ensuring closeness to their god.

Martin wondered whether the ancient world in general, and the world of the Pharaohs specifically, recognized the connection between birth defects, physical and mental, and marriage within the family. It was quite possible that they did not. Obviously, it was not possible to completely guard the purity of the family bloodline. There were times when the institution of marriage was influenced by political considerations. Amenhotep III entered into a political marriage with Tadukhipa, daughter of the king of Mitanni, in northern Syria. When Amenhotep III died, the prince, Amenhotep IV, inherited Tadukhipa, who became his wife and carnal partner. The writings of El-Armana, researched diligently by Dr. Martin Klopstock, included various testimonies about daughters of foreign kings brought to Egypt to marry Pharaohs, but he found no sign of Egyptian kings sending their daughters to marry other leaders. This discrepancy is one of the pieces of evidence pointing to the clear supremacy of Egypt among its neighbors.

Dr. Martin Klopstock was aware that among the intellectuals of his time the belief was prevalent that there were two types of researchers. The first type was introverted. The introverts preferred to take part only in scientific activities and limited as much as possible any necessary secondary pursuits. The second type, the extroverts, enjoyed the world surrounding their research. The second type like to "take care of business", and often their advancement surpassed those of the first type since they knew how to forge secondary paths to their promotion. The extroverts saw the introverts as having characteristics of field mice who focus solely on what is theirs, and the introverts also saw the extroverts as a type of mouse – one that runs hither and yon, depleting its energy by giving too much credence to juicy gossip, spending too much time on useless activities, and enjoying circulating rumors.

Martin had the "soul of an archeologist" and was as familiar with the realities of ancient Egypt as he was the modern views of the world. He did not neglect to study the scandal that was called in those days "The curse of the Pharaohs." Martin knew it well in all of its aspects.

Years after the discovery of the bust of Nefertiti in Egypt in 1912 by German archeologist Ludwig Borchardt, the world found itself entering into a frightful spiral of fear and dogma. In ancient tradition, the cobra snake was assigned the task of guarding the entrances to the Pharaoh's tombs against intruders, burglary and pilfering. In 1922, the tomb of Tutankhamun was uncovered in the Valley of the Kings. Soon afterward, the story was circulated that a cobra had swallowed a pet canary belonging to Howard Carter, the senior archeologist in the party that discovered the tomb. The British press took up the story of the hapless canary and reported to readers that next to the ancient graves were found inscriptions with mysterious significance such as "He shall die who passed this threshold," and "Bitterly punished shall be he who breaks into these graves." One of the inscriptions, so it was told, was found at the foot of the statue of Anubis, a god wi,th the head of a jackal who, according to Egyptian mythology, stood guard over the graves.

The aura that the story created was further enhanced by a series of mysterious deaths that occurred within a short period. The blows were inflicted mostly upon members of the inner circle around the discoverer of the tomb. Carter's assistant died suddenly while emptying the tomb, and Carter's secretary died of unknown causes while taking a bath, and the secretary's father committed suicide. An x-ray technician, on his way to Egypt to examine the mummy, died before he arrived at his destination.

Carter, of course, had a hard time getting over the death of his canary in the throat of the snake, but, with hindsight, the "curse of the Pharaohs" fanned the flames of public interest in his discovery and aggrandized the importance of his work. Perhaps this is why Martin saw no evidence of resistance on the part of Carter to the publishing of stories of the "Curse of the Pharaohs". Indeed there was an interesting human-interest story woven through the subject.

During this same time period, Boris Karloff, of Hollywood horror film fame, reached new artistic heights. His sense of drama was fed by the mysterious stories coming from the Valley of the Kings. He sent chills up the spines of millions of Americans with his depiction of a mummy buried in the Valley of the Kings being disturbed by some fellows having not a shred of manners. In the movie, the mummy has its revenge upon the gutsy archeologists who dare to invade his tomb.

The US Senate voted on the formation of an independent committee of investigation, one not comprised of politicians whose scientific knowledge was spoon-fed to them by gifted, unscrupulous lobbyists. The committee was to decide whether the importation of mummies to be displayed in American museums presented a threat in the form of dangerous microbes.

While this was taking place, Martin was stricken with a cold and he let it be known time and again that he had no intention of wasting any of his time on such an outrage. He refused to answer any questions from journalists. He knew very well the widespread speculation about the source of the "Curse of the Pharaohs". As a dedicated German he believed that the British, out of jealousy over the discovery by the Germans of the bust of Nefertiti, decided to try to increase the apparent importance of their discovery of the tomb of Tutankhamun, and to that end they were spreading the myth of the "curse".

We must not forget that they were also influenced by the rivalries of WWI.

Martin was unable to find an actual source of the frightening inscriptions from the time of the Pharaohs. He searched for them on the outer and inner walls of the tombs, and on the ancient statues. He tended to believe that they were modern day inventions to suit a purpose. As a loyal German, believed the contention that the "Curse of the Pharaohs" was a trick by the British meant to scare unwanted competition – the Germans and reporters – away from the tomb of Tutankhamun. To accomplish this, the British archeologists recruited the author Arthur Conan Doyle, creator of the character Sherlock Holmes, to the cause. Doyle wrote stories about the magic powers of the priests of Tutankhamun who created "natural means" of guarding the tombs. The jump from there to the idea that mortally dangerous bacteria were the guardians of the tombs was but a short one.

Chapter Seven:
The royal visit

When King Akhenaton noticed that his wife was spending most of her time on the water, and that it seemed his company was not particularly required, he asked her,

"My dear, would you like me to join you on a trip on the great river?"

"Of course, if you would like to, my love", she quickly answered.

His next question came as a great surprise. "I am considering a journey to tour the region of Thebes. We can sail there on a boat, and then continue on dry land in various directions from the port. Does this interest you?"

"You? Thebes? What brings you to want to visit the city you left?" she asked in amazement.

"Surely you remember that before we moved here, to Akhetaton, I built a temple called Gempaaten, which means 'The sun disk is found in the estate of the God Aton'. I built it from small stones, their size approximating that of the head of human being, allowing rapid construction. I am curious to see what has become of that temple."

Nefertiti liked the idea. "Absolutely. I am very happy that you suggested this. I have not yet paid a visit to Karnak or Luxor, nor have I yet visited the Valley of the Kings' tombs, that lies on the other side of the river."

When he became king, Akhenaton stopped practicing any of the rites associated with the old religion that were the norm during the times preceding his rule. Under the old religion it was customary for relatives of the deceased to visit their tombs each year and hold prayer ceremonies. They opened the eyes of the dead person, and removed the plugs from his ears and mouth so that he could participate in the event by tasting the food and drink they had brought each time they came to the grave.

She looked at him with wonder, "I'm not sure why you continue to take an interest in the temple at Thebes, since you have established Akhetaton."

He smiled at her and responded, "I will tell you the truth. It is not the temple of Gempaaten that interests me. It is the hall of giant pylons at the site of Amon-Ra at Karnak that I really wish to see."

"You miss it?" she asked with a smile.

"Yes I do. There is nothing grander in the kingdom than that temple. Even the pyramids at Giza could not compete with the inspiration its proportions provide men who walk among its columns. I am repelled by the religion, as you know, but they had good engineers who knew how to build."

"Yes, I too like the giant hall and I've had already had the opportunity to take in the impressive sight of it. We Egyptians do like things large. It shows who we are," said Nefertiti, and she quite enjoyed uttering those words.

"The hall contains one hundred and thirty-four massive columns arranged in sixteen rows. The height of one hundred and twenty two of them is equal to five and a half men standing one on top of the head of the other. Each of the remaining twelve columns is twice that height. The diameter of each column is equal to two men lying at their full length with the head of one against the feet of the other," said Akhenaton.

"I remember none of this. How interesting that you manage to remember all of the details," she said.

"More interesting is the fact that the building of the structure took place over an extended period of time, and despite disagreements between the Pharaohs of all the generations, perhaps thirty of them, they managed to maintain amazing architectural harmony."

Akhenaton knew the explanation for this. It stemmed from engineering considerations. The building of the massive, flat roofs of the shrines demanded solid support. For this the thick external walls were helpful, especially the crowded columns (the arch had not yet been invented.) Lotus and papyrus decorative patterns repeated themselves throughout the generations. Akhenaton chose not to discuss the conservative aspects of Egyptian buildings with his wife. He understood their value, but he was a man always looking for the new. As opposed to those mysterious shrines of darkness, the temples he preferred were those where Aton was worshipped in the direct sunlight.

They were both well aware that in addition to

being places of worship, the temples played a central economic role. They were used to store the treasure troves of crops and money and they served as a base for the state to control its citizenry.

"As you said, a great tradition of talented engineers," she agreed with him. "It's particularly difficult for me to grasp how they managed to lift the pillars, weighing such unthinkable amounts, to such unfathomable heights…"

Her husband attempted to explain. "You likely recall that at the top of each column there is a very large architrave weighing nearly as much as a large boat. Raising those up to the top of such tall columns and setting them precisely in place was a difficult feat indeed," he said. He then immediately continued, "The structures were raised with the help of embankments that were built out of large boulders. The spaces between the boulders were filled with mud bricks. Each architrave was hoisted up along the resulting long slanting ramp. At the conclusion of the work, the embankment was discarded."

"I just don't understand where they found the patience for such a protracted project", said Nefertiti.

"You will be glad to know that there are people who differ from you," answered Akhenaton curtly.

Dr. Klopstock's notebooks contained his conflicting thoughts on the subject of the patience exhibited by the Pharaohs during the construction of the magnificent temples that took generations to complete. He also thought about the builders of the great cathedrals of Europe about two thousand years later that also sometimes took hundreds of years to finish. In Europe, during those times styles changed often, whereas in ancient Egypt the same style prevailed throughout long periods of history. In Martin's notebook, special attention was paid to the changes in architectural style that took place over time in Europe. These changes were reflected in the Chartre Cathedral in France. Martin's research notebook contained various sketches of the structure of the cathedral as it changed over time. The cathedral already existed in the fifth century, built in an undefined Roman style. In the eleventh and twelfth centuries it was changed to the massive Romanesque style, characterized by thick walls and columns, towers, arcades, and round arches. Near the end of this period, the front of the building was rebuilt in early Gothic style. The cathedral was destroyed by fire at the end of the twelfth century, and its reconstruction, ending in the year 1220, was done in pronounced high Gothic mode.

Of course we can't compare the architectural styles of Egypt and France, but Martin got caught up in thinking about the European cathedrals in an effort to understand the human motivation to satisfy religious needs that beat in the hearts of those who worked on the construction of these religious buildings during the various time periods. These internal drives of the soul are what brought about extremism - so different from the usual human experience. It seemed that this powerful internal pressure felt by servants of religion, including the high clergy and the various kings over generations, had not changed for thousands of years.

Perhaps this pressure is the instinct for argumentation and dispute. The Pharaohs competed among themselves to build the most magnificent edifice. It was a "catch as you can" kind of rivalry in a time when the destruction of a previously built structure and the use of it as a source of ready raw materials were seen as quite legitimate. The kings of Europe were busy widening their empires all over the globe. Spain reached all the way to Peru, and Britain embraced Australia. Martin was not mistaken in what he wrote. He could know that in the future rulers in Hong Kong and Shanghai would quarrel over who had built the tallest hotel in the world, or that powerful leaders would conceal and cover up upsetting events in the past and present in order to be seen as the "most democratic". This did not differ from the competition among scientists over who was first to discover something or other, nor was it different from the ambitions of reporters bickering over who was the first to turn the latest gossip into a "scoop".

Martin's research revealed support for his contention that after the royal couple visited the hall of the amazing pylons in Karnak, they crossed the river to the western side and continued their journey with a visit to the "Valley of the Kings", a name more esthetically pleasing than "Valley of Death". This valley, on the western bank, was completely different than the eastern bank. It totally lacked the trees and green vegetation that surrounded the villages where the Egyptian people dwelled. The western side of the river was dominated by expanses of sand and stone, at the mercy of the wind and the blazing sun. The only permanent residents of this part of Egypt were the workers who took part in the building of the tombs of the kings. In addition to the laborers, there were the very talented royal artisans who filled the tombs with their immortal creations. They and their families were isolated from the rest of the world, and never crossed the river to the eastern side. They were denied this freedom so as to prevent any knowledge of the fantastic treasures that were entombed with the mummies from being passed to those in the land of the living. This was a cruel bondage, believed to prevent theft from the graves.

Dr. Martin Klopstock was most familiar with this holy valley in which were interred thirty kings, including the most prominent Pharaohs of ancient Egypt. Thutmose III was among them. Martin, along with the world, mourned the fact that despite all efforts to prevent pillage of the tombs, most of them had been opened and the sanctity of the deceased had been defiled.

As they crossed the river on their way to the western land, Akhenaton prepared Nefertiti for the wondrous sights that awaited them. He spoke especially about the amazing murals that filled the inner walls of the tombs, depicting the journey of the kings in through the underworld. These illustrations were joined by passages from the Book of the Dead, intended to strengthen the souls of those passing from one world to the next when they would stand in judgment before the gods.

"If the tombs have not been plundered, we'll be able to see the abundance that surrounds the coffins of the mummies who lie at rest on their backs. The treasure is there to ensure their lives will be eternally enriched in the next world," the king explained to his wife.

"Do you really believe in all of that?" Nefertiti came back with the question.

"Why not? After all, it's what we've believed for many hundreds of years. Were it not true, someone would surely have discovered it by this time," he answered.

"Perhaps nobody ever thought deeply about this in the past. They simply lived their lives without asking questions. As far as I know, you are the first person since I've been aware of what goes on among you Egyptians, who has asked difficult questions about the existence of god. Nor have I ever come across such questioning in my country, Mittani." Her worlds sounded factual, but ended with a shade of wonder.

A long period of silence followed as doubts festered in both of their hearts.

We should visit the Temple of Death that my father built. What is mainly of interest there are the two giant statues that stand at the entrance to the temple. The statues are made from boulders my father had mined near Cairo and brought over the river on sailing ships.

I can tell you that bringing these rocks cost him much difficulty. Several boats had to be tied to one another in order to load the gigantic, massive boulders that were heavier perhaps that than any load shipped on the river by any previous Egyptian king.", said Akhenaton.

Dr. Klopstock wrote may notes, especially on the matter of these two statues (called "The Collasi of Memnon", in singular, "collasus", meaning a giant statue) and he noted their great height of seventeen meters. He wrote in his notebook:

"The boulders from which the statues were carved were small quartz crystals held togcthcr by a binding material, apparently limestone. Over the years the binding material was damaged, causing some of the crystals to be loosened and to become separated from the statues. The original shape of the statues was thus compromised, at least in part. Research later showed that the ancient Greeks who visited the place several hundred years after the time of the Pharaohs, dedicated the statues in the name of Memnon of Troy who blessed his mother each morning with song. They discovered that when the sunlight of dawn each morning warmed the quartz crystals, they expanded, and tension was created within the structure of the statues. This caused the statues to make sounds that to the Greeks sounded like moaning, which they equated to the song of Memnon. In the vicinity of the giant statues were found only a few remnants of the Temple of Death built by Amenhotep III, in the form of several sphinxes missing their heads." Martin pointed out in his notes that today it's difficult to discern whether there had or had not been additional gigantic statues at this site.

Nefertiti was very impressed by the two enormous statues. They represented giant Pharaohs sitting with pride on their royal throne. "Seeing them sit so assuredly upon the seat of power forms within me a feeling of great security about the continuation of the Egyptian monarchy," she said to Akhenaton.

"That is apparently the way my father felt when he ordered the erection of the statues. As you know, the bloated and rotting religious priesthood in Thebes instilled doubt in my heart as to the future stability of the kingdom, and that is why I moved the capitol to Akhetaton and undertook the establishment of a new, more streamlined clergy," answered her husband. "Actually, the priests were already causing my father concern but he was busy with war, and did not have time to deal with them until I arrived and did what had to be done."

Nefertiti felt the obvious pride in his words, and he did not try to hide it. There was not much new in what he said since he had often repeated these words in previous conversations, but this time she listened.

For Akhenaton, the last phase of the royal visit was the most important. This was in the section of the valley containing the tombs of the kings of the new kingdom of the eighteenth dynasty, beginning with the Pharaoh Thutmose I. It was well known in the days of Akhenaton that the tombs had been stricken by robberies. The serious punishment received by those caught in the offense, which was considered most heinous, did not deter the sophisticated thieves who became rich from the spoils of their crime. Among other things, Akhenaton took an interest in the methods used in the Valley of the Kings to prevent penetration of the tombs of the Pharaoh.

"I'm having trouble deciding," he said to Nefertiti as the two stood before the tomb of the Pharaoh Thutmose I, "whether we should be interred here at the end of our days, or would it be preferable to build a new Valley of the Kings near us, in Akhetaton. What is your opinion?"

It was a complicated question, and it surprised her.

"Wow," she said. "A difficult question for one morning."

"Where would you prefer me to lie in my coffin? Here, or at home?" he reformulated the question.

"Are you trying to suggest that one day you will have to join this group?" she asked with a smile and waved her hand in the direction of the tombs of the Pharaohs in front of her.

"Perhaps that day will come," he answered her, his face serious. She knew that expression from moments when he would deliver an off-color joke when no stranger was within hearing. They both burst into ringing laughter that belonged to the royal couple alone.

Akhenaton and Nefertiti stopped laughing and became engrossed in deep thought. They stayed silent a long while. At last he said, "I prefer to be buried in our area when the time comes. When we return to the castle, I will start to work with my engineers on the new Valley of the Kings at Akhenaton."

These words, too, he delivered with seriousness – a different kind of seriousness this time.

"I will be entombed wherever you choose," she told him, which gave him great pleasure. In her heart she believed that she would outlive him, and the place of her burial would surely be influenced by developments that were beyond her power to predict.

After another silence she asked, "Why did you not tell me - not at the beginning of our visit to the temple that you built at Thebes, and not during our visit to the temple of the pylons, and not here in the Valley of the Kings, that the main reason for this tour was your desire to make a decision about the building of a new Valley of the Kings in Akhetaton?"

His face grew serious yet again as he answered, "That was not the most important reason for our tip to the south. I wanted to get an impression of the great temple at Karnak before I decide whether we want to build something of such proportions in Akhetaton. The idea for a new Valley of the Kings came to me while we were here." He sounded convincing and she tended to believe him, even though some doubts remained that she chose not to bring up.

Dr. Klopstock endeavored to investigate the relationship between the king and queen in order to identify the turning point at which a distance began to form between them. During the first years of their marriage they had become very close, physically as well as emotionally. In those years Akhenaton would ask Nefertiti's counsel before making important decisions.

Chapter Eight:
Bringing Up Daughters

Insofar as it is possible to imagine the palace lifestyle, it would seem that Nefertiti had a rather normal family life. She and Akhenaton had six daughters. Each of them had her own separate governess who brought up her princess in the manner befitting a daughter of the queen. We do not know of the fates of the five other daughters, but we know that the third daughter, Ankhensenpaaten, was different than her sisters. Even as a young child, Ankhensepaaten was known for having a distinctive personality. She was unstable in her opinions, preferences, and behaviors. She was rebellious toward her governess, and sometimes her mother, Nefertiti, was called upon to intervene.

As the years went by and Ankhensepaaten passed from childhood to adolescence and became a beautiful young woman, her characteristic snobbishness and conceit stood out. She closely resembled her mother, and she would often say as much to everyone, receiving validation from all who came into the court of the king, even those not involved in the intrigues of the royal household.

Nefertiti may have expected Ankhesenpaaten to be her successor. Perhaps because of her daughter's difficulty at conforming to the strict rules of palace life, or for other reasons, the mother felt a special closeness to her stormy daughter, and she tried to help Ankhesenpaaten bridge the raging waters of life. For the most part she did not succeed.

"Your governess informs me that every time she tries to help you, she is met with hostile resistance. She tells you to do something and you try to do the exact opposite. That is not a good way to succeed in life," Ankhesenpaaten's mother tried to explain to her. The girl refused to listen to Nefertiti's admonitions. She answered off-handedly, "Don't listen to anything she tells you about me."

The members of the royal household did not consider themselves "spoiled", although spending most of their time in the pursuit of life's pleasures was a large part of their lifestyle. And in this not only was Ankhesenpaaten very active, but she exceeded the others many times over. Whatever clothing she put on in the morning would be changed in the afternoon, and yet again in the evening. Some days she would change even more often, since Ankhesenpaaten was often of a different mind late in the morning than she had been early in the morning.

One day her mother said, "Ankhesenpaaten, my dear, I have never seen such selfish behavior. Where did you acquire these self-centered tendencies?"

The answer Nefertiti received was "What can I do, Mother? This is just the way I am – a selfish character – I was born this way. It can't be helped!"

"What do you mean what can you do? You can, and you must, try to behave more like a human being.

Sometimes you have to think of those around you, and try to help them."

"I've tried that and it didn't work for me," said Ankhesenpaaten.

"Then you didn't try hard enough. Do you think you'll be able to get a husband who will love you and keep you for himself and who will not want to throw you into the great river when all you have to offer him is your selfishness?"

"Selfishness is not all that I have to offer. You know that better than I," the daughter answered, winking at her mother with her well made-up eyes.

"Your beauty, if that is what you mean, is not enough. Don't delude yourself," said Nefertiti.

The queen often thought, and asked aloud, "where did I go wrong in the education of the daughter who is especially close to my heart? I had have heard much about the difficulties in bringing up children that were experienced by royal families in the past, but I never imagined that even in these modern times a mother could intend a particular result and get its opposite, even when she gives her daughter everything she needs."

In time it became clear that the mother was correct. Ankhesenpaaten became the wife of Tuthankhamun, but he despised her, and he took Ankhesenamun as his queen. According to the later notebook of Dr. Klopstock, (the one written after World War II), in the year 1332 B.C. the two were married, and an everlasting picture of the young Ankhesenamun and Tuthankhamun, appearing side by side in magnificent harmony, adorns the armrest of the golden throne found inside the tomb of Thutankhamun.

Chapter Nine:
Homecoming

The royal vessel sailed northward on the waters of the river, toward home. The king and queen had ended yesterday's tour later than planned, getting back to the boat in darkness, quite tired. They usually went to bed early and were early to rise. Nefertiti enjoyed standing near the pointed bow and looking at the wake. Sometimes she would bend down over the railing in hopes of feeling drops of moisture from the spray. This didn't happen when the river was calm since the deck was high above the water level, but from time to time, when the water was rough and the bow of the boat pierced a lofty wave, she got a pleasant shower on her face.

During the first week of the royal couple's sailing trip southward to Thebes, the king had usually preferred to sit in the back of the vessel, near his work desk where all of the documents that had been brought on board at his request were kept. There were various documents engraved in soft chalk stone or carved in limestone, and there were some written on parchment. A few especially important documents were engraved in hard basalt or granite, and tablets that had been brought from distant Mesopotamia were molded from clay. The desk of Akhenaton held items from the royal archive. When the king wished to look at these materials he sent for the royal interpreter who sailed with the party, to translate the written Accadian language.

But the first morning of their northward sail toward home, Akhenaton joined his wife at the bow of the boat. They wrapped themselves in silky cloaks against the cool dawn air that chilled their bodies right through their light clothing. They both looked very beautiful.

"What a pleasure for me to behold your loveliness this morning," he told her. The king placed his arm on her shoulder and lightly pulled her toward him. Nefertiti lifted her head and smiled. "You are happy with me?" she asked.

"Yes. Very happy," he answered.

"We must take more trips together on the river. Perhaps you'll be able to free more time from your work and come with me to experience what the river affords those who love it?" she asked.

"I wish I could. Unfortunately there is much work waiting for me that does not allow the pleasure you are suggesting," he responded.

"But you have been working every day of the trip," she argued, "why don't you try to do this more often?"

"Perhaps, we'll see", was his answer.

The king was satisfied with the visits they had made in the region of Thebes. In each place they landed they had received adoration and respect when they came ashore, and the local officials had given them generous gifts. "The Egyptians are a good people", repeated Nefertiti many times during their tour. "I am happy that we took this trip," answered her husband.

Dr. Klopstock came to the conclusion that during the period of their visit to Thebes, the relationship between Akhenaton and his wife the queen had been a strong one. Martin had pondered whether this was true in light of the many trips the queen had taken on the royal boat while her husband stayed on land and focused on the work of erecting the new city. His suspicions had mainly centered around the faithfulness of the queen when she invited the multi-talented Thutmose to join her in sailing the river so that he could continue to sculpt her image. It would seem that physical intimacy had not yet occurred between the artist and the queen, although there was no certainty that an emotional bond of some kind had not been formed.

Martin was careful not to let his Judaism affect his perceptions with regard to the religious developments during the time of Akhenaton, but he couldn't help having some special feelings about the subject, and he took particular interest in all that had to do with the "monotheism" of the time, and it's central part in the Old Testament. During the earliest phases of his research, Martin looked at the fact that Akhenaton had been favored for the kingship despite his being the younger of two brothers. The elder brother had contracted an illness from which he never recovered, and the younger had assumed his place as Amenhotep IV. This was a case of the biblical "sibling rivalry" that began with Kane and Abel, continued with Isaac and Ishmael, Jacob and Esau, Joseph and his brothers Ephraim and Menashe, and now repeated itself with the heirs of Amenhotep III. Was this only coincidence? Could not this similarity of preference point to a certain divine philosophy? This is what Martin asked himself.

The question of monotheism intrigued Martin for another reason as well. The writings of El Amarna mentioned the Apriu, thought to be Canaanite tribes living during the time of El Amarna. His curiosity was piqued further by the similarity between "apar" and "avar", since the connection between the ancient letters for "p" and "b" in the ancient languages was already documented. This comparison contradicted another language development regarding the tribes called the "Habiru". The similarity between this and "Hebrews" also got Martin's attention. The term "Habiru" in those days was negatively linked to the outcast groups or robbers in the margins of society of other nations. The story goes that they offered their services as mercenaries to princes and kings, just as did David and Yiftach from the old testament, during times of strife.

Another interesting explanation of the link between the terms is based on the similarity between the descriptions that appear in ancient writings, in which the "Habiru" is described as a tribe of slaves during the time of the building of the Pharaoh's temples, and the descriptions of the people of Israel as slaves in Egypt in the Book of Exodus.

Time calculations place Joseph, son of Jacob, and Akhenaton as having lived at the same time. So was it the many-talented Joseph who, during his time in Egypt, influenced Akhenaton adopt the belief if one god?

Martin did not believe this theory. Unlike Thutmose, creator of the bust of Nefertiti, who saw his queen as having no interest in religion, Martin was of the opinion that Akhenaton actually got his religious tendencies from Nefertiti. Her Mittani origins meant that she and her childhood family had come into contact with monotheistic ideas in their homeland. Mittani was an ancient kingdom in northern Mesopotamia (today northern Iraq and eastern Syria), the center of which was the upper Tigres and Euphrates area, known also as Naharayim, which is the region where Abraham and his family lived. There they came to comprehend the idea of monotheism even before they went to the land of Canaan.

Dr. Klopstock wrote quite a bit in his notebook about the visit Akhenaton and his wife made to the Valley of the Kings. The valley symbolized the death that brings with it a change that sometimes meant a complete overturning of a regime. Immediately following the death of Akhenaton, the city of Akhetaton, the seat of Amarna, was abandoned and turned to rubble. Martin was taken aback by what characterized the meteoric rise and just as rapid fall of monotheism in ancient Egypt - the hatred, loathing, and vindictiveness felt by those who strove to erase the name of Akhenaton from the history of Egypt. It was hard for him to identify the most significant cause that fueled that hatred and hostility.

Was it the relocation of the capitol from one place to another? The cutting off of the priests of Ra-Amon from their sources of wealth and authority? Or was it the new religion and the image of the new god? Or perhaps the main reasons for his indictment were Akhenaton's bold decision not to recognize the importance of the existing customs, and his desire to implement profound shifts from the familiar reality.

The list is long of others in history that fell to bitter ends for putting their faith in new and different truths that were revealed to them, and for wanting their discoveries to become known by everyone. Why was the Italian Giordano Bruno burned at the stake in 1600 if not for airing his opinions that went against those of the rulers at the time? And what about Galileo Galilei, who almost lost his life so many years later when he repeated Akhenaton's heliocentric assertion that the earth and other planets, including Jupiter and its four moons, revolve around the sun? Even Jesus Christ belonged on this list.

Martin was reminded of Joseph, son of Jacob, who came to Egypt and even ruled over it, yet nevertheless remained an outsider. He wrought fundamental changes in the economic system of the country that accepted him according to ancient dictates. Perhaps if he had been born a native Egyptian son, he would not have found the courage and the inner drive to bring about the revolution that took place in Egypt. And Martin knew very well the names of the Jewish leaders who surrounded Lenin at the time of his Bolshevik revolution. They were supposedly Russian, but of a separate kind. Did not all of these have something in common?

Indeed, the Jews wandered from country to country, and brought changes in regime to every new place. Yet the Jews remained strangers in each place they went, and suffered the hatred that natives have for newcomers.

A short time after the royal couple returned to Akhetaton, the artist Thutmose was summoned to the palace to continue his work on the bust of Nefertiti.

"Have you had enough of a break from me?" she asked him.

"Actually I missed Her Majesty the Queen," he said with pent up emotion.

She was pleased with his answer and responded with a mischievous smile, "Well, you needn't exaggerate." Thutmose thought her remark too casual, and he did not know about what he should try not to exaggerate.

From this portion of their interaction Dr. Klopstock understood that physical distance between the artist and the queen was still being maintained, although perhaps there had been some initial attempts at closeness between the two even before her trip to Thebes.

It is possible that during this period of time an attachment was developing between Akhenaton and the woman who would later become Queen Kiya, but there was still no official relationship between the two.

Several months later, the content of the conversation between Nefertiti and her sculptor changed. "You promised that I would be the most beautiful woman in the world," Nefertiti reminded him.

"Indeed, my queen, I did promise, and I kept that promise. In the most prestigious place in the palace, right next to the king's golden throne, stands the bust that you chose from among all of the statues I made of your image," Thutmose answered carefully.

"That is true. But I ask myself if you could not, with a bit more effort, make something even more perfect," she told him.

"I will do my utmost, honorable queen," he answered. His heart leapt at the Queen's suggestion. The requested resumption of their work together gave him the opportunity for many more visits to the palace, and a continuation of the prestigious status he had acquired among the subjects of the king and queen.

The queen was not sure what nature of relationship she desired to create between them. She enjoyed hearing him call her "Your Majesty the Queen", however this expression formed a certain barrier between them, and she wanted to know this man with no barriers. Though her husband was trying to keep it from her, she already knew that Kiya was about to become his wife, and also knew that she had nothing to say in the matter. Nefertiti believed that when Akhenaton tired of Kiya, he would come back to her. Kiya may have been the younger of the two women, but there was no comparison to be made between the radiantly beautiful Nefertiti and the moon-faced Kiya.

Nefertiti knew that one could never predict how things would develop. She was known as, and would always be known as, the first queen. This title could never be stripped from her. However, she did not wish to appear at official royal ceremonies while another woman was warming the king's couch. Even though he was not the most attractive of men when it came to bedroom matters, she insisted on being afforded the respect a woman deserved. And she was not just any woman, but the most desirable woman in the world. She definitely did not want a situation whereby in the royal court, and afterwards in the streets, there would be whispers that her charm had vanished and her womb was dry.

Nefertiti sat in front of Thutmose and he gazed at her face. She looked at his face as well and at his muscular arms. She did not understand why she had to keep sitting for him day after day. By now surely he knew what she looked like and he did not have to come back each day after working long hours during the weeks leading up to the trip on the river. The look of her face and her features must by now be engraved in his mind as well as drawn on the parchment he used for sketches and notes. So, why did he continue to gaze at her and to draw more depictions of her body on the parchment? Perhaps he had other intentions toward her? He was a man like all other men, after all. Set a trap for them, and they will, without a doubt, fall into it.

He may have guessed at her thoughts. If she wanted

to move them in a bold direction, she would have to take the first step. Women usually have ways in which they initiate the turning of a relationship toward romance. In this case, there was not doubt that she would need to be the first to cross the line. There was a kind of tension between them. They both felt the electricity in the air.

"Have you had intimate relations with any of the women in the palace?" she asked him.

"No, my qeen," he answered.

"Would you like to have such relations?" she asked him.

Thutmose decided not to answer this provocative question. He stopped working for a few seconds and then started again.

"Did you understand my question?"

"Yes, I understood your Majesty" was his answer.

"Then why do you not answer me?" she asked.

He remained silent.

"Come closer to me," she said. "Put your hands on my face."

He complied with her request. "Is my face warm?" she asked.

"Yes," was the answer.

"Too warm?"

"Yes," he answered.

She placed her hands on his face and said, "Your face is very warm as well."

He was silent.

"What does it mean that our faces are so warm?"

"That we have warm faces," he said.

"Idiot," she answered, and pressed her lips on his mouth. Not stopping her, he wrapped her in his arms and held her to his chest. When they drew apart she said, "You are very good at that."

He answered, "You have yet no idea what goodness I can provide."

"What will you say to your wife if one day she tells you she knows of your relations with me?" she asked him suddenly.

He found it hard to answer. "Of course, you will tell her it's only gossip of the sort that it's impossible to prevent around the palace," she tried to help him.

"And if she doesn't believe me?" he tried to place himself into the scenario she'd created.

"Then perhaps you must insist. She does not have to know everything that happens in the palace," explained Nefertiti.

"I myself do not know everything that happens in the palace. You too may not know all that occurs in this huge complex." He tried gently to lesson the sting of the wound her remarks had made.

"Do you have a better idea?" she asked him, becoming slightly angry.

This was the meeting in which they consummated their intimate relationship, but there was still a distance between them that had not yet been traversed.

The more he tried to penetrate the depths of the souls of his ancient heroes, the more Martin felt an urge to deviate from his central research on the bust of Nefertiti. Periodic breaks from the "Nefertiti routine" in order to temporarily pursue other artistic subjects helped him keep the intellectual equilibrium so necessary to a scientist such as himself. Otherwise, he thought, he might become entwined emotionally in the personal lives of the queen and the sculptor, Thutmose, who was involved with Nefertiti beyond the artistic aspects of the work.

With this in mind, Martin took up some studies of things unrelated to his main area of research. Besides the temples, the palaces, and the other artistry to the gods that the Pharaohs erected, the furnishings used by the kings also fascinated Dr. Klopstock. Without a doubt, one of the most fascinating pieces was the throne of Tutankhamun, found near the mummy, preserved in an astonishing way – it was covered in gold. On the backrest of the throne appeared a surprisingly natural picture of the royal couple, King Thutankhamun and his wife, Ankesenaamen. In the picture, he is seated on the throne in a relaxed position, and she stands before him with her right hand gently touching his left shoulder. The armrests of the throne end in lions' heads meant to protect the king, so that when he stretched out his arms his hands rested on the beasts' heads. The bottoms of the four legs of the king's throne were carved into the shape of an animal's hooves.

As an expert in the furnishings of royal homes, Dr. Klopstock appreciated the influence the Pharaoh's throne had on the design of furniture in later generations. Simple comparison showed that the furniture designers in Europe at the beginning of the eighteenth century used important basic elements from the throne of Tutenkhamun in the style called "Queen Anne". The ornate Queen Anne chairs had rounded legs that ended in carved animal hooves at the bottom.

While Dr. Klopstock studied the influence of the Pharaoh Tutankhamun's throne on Queen Anne style furniture, he often looked up with pleasure at the large picture of the king's golden throne that hung above his desk.

Chapter Ten:
Potsdam

The Klopstocks belonged to an old family that had been well known in Potsdam for generations. They were proud of the fact that their family patriarch, Klaus Kloptstock, had come to Potsdam after the Thirty Years War in the mid 17th century. Ironically, though it was a passionate war in which Catholics fought with all their might against the Protestants in unrelenting battles all over Europe that claimed many victims, the Jewish family managed to survive and find shelter in Potsdam. This turned out to be quite a comfortable period of time for those seeking to settle and make their futures in Potsdam. The Kingdom of Prussia encouraged this settlement and offered immigrants from all over Europe the services of the developing city. In hopes that this policy would help turn Potsdam into an international metropolis, it included complete freedom of religion, exemptions from taxes, and benefits for land purchasers.

Over the years, the Klopstock family was respectably represented in the various cultural spheres of the city. The family included physicians and affluent merchants as well as artists. One of the most prominent among them was the landscape architect, Peter Klopstock who planned and built some of the famous parks and gardens of Potsdam, designed in various European styles, Peter's preference being for the French style.

Martin Klopstock decided that there were already enough doctors and lawyers in the family. He liked archeology, and as was expected of him, was an excellent student. To make a living during his time as a University student, he became a tour guide for visitors to Potsdam, and came to know every structure in his city that had any architectural artistic value. He was also well versed in the history of the various buildings of his birth city. Martin was especially knowledgeable about all of the hidden waterways and reservoirs that were connected to one another in Potsdam, and he showed these to the tourists he guided.

Martin made sure that importance was placed during his tours on familiarity with the royal buildings in the city, among them being the Palace of Sanssouci (In French: "having no worries"). Most of these were built by King Frederick II, known as "Frederick the Great." His reign lasted thirty six years and his accomplishments won much recognition. Martin admired King Frederick the Great, since much of the city's special beauty was to his credit.

Potsdam developed into one of the most important centers of the moving picture industry on the European continent. (The Klopstock family's contribution to that industry was the director Yohann Klopstock). Potsdam's biggest competitor in the tourism arena was nearby Berlin. The two cities were only thirty kilometers apart, but Potsdam outdid Berlin with its palaces, parks, and museums. Martin attributed Potsdam's advantage to the Hohenzollern family that ruled over Prussia and made the decision to turn Potsdam into the capitol of the country.

But beauty is fleeting. In the 18th century the Hohenzollem family decided that Potsdam was to become the military seat of the county, and military administration buildings and barracks began to dominate the city. Also, in contrast to Martin's city, Berlin was increasing its economic strength. When Martin finished his studies, he stopped working as a tour guide and went to work in Berlin, where he got a job at a museum that specialized in archeology.

Dr. Martin Klopstock and his family continued to thrive and flourish in Potsdam until 1933, when the Nazis rose to power. During the following few years the family fell apart. Some of its members moved to England, some tried their luck at success in the United States of America, and there were Klopstocks who went to Israel.

Martin and his brother Max decided not to uproot their families, and to remain in the land of their birth. Max was a well-to-do man who owned agricultural land in several areas of the province of Brandenburg. When Martin was dismissed from his job at the museum in Berlin, the two brothers moved their families into adjoining farms belonging to Max, and they made a modest living from the land. They tried not to leave the confines of their property and lived off the fruit of their labor. The farms provided them an abundance of vegetables, fruit, milk, and meat and they lacked for nothing. They educated their children at home. Martin, Max, and their families looked Arian, and none of their neighbors suspected that they were not of the pure German race.

When they needed to make special purchases, visit a doctor, or do their banking, they would travel to Berlin. They preferred to take care of these errands in the big city and to limit their visits to Potsdam so as not to bump into acquaintances.

In Dr. Klopstock's sheaf of notebooks, discovered after the Second World War, he had recorded the conversations he had with his brother Max during the time they lived on the land together after the Nazis had come to power.

"How long do you think we will have to hide here?" Martin asked Max one day.

"That's hard to say. Perhaps a few more months, or a year, or at most until the next election," answered Martin. "It is hard to believe that people will continue to suffer that crazy man for very much longer."

"I notice that people actually like him more and more as time goes on," Max expressed his opinion.

"The people who like him are the former nothings who have suddenly become important managers," said Martin.

"They are the most dangerous and we must be on our guard against them," agreed Max. "When I walk in the street and see the swastika on someone's arm, I try to keep my distance, of course without arousing suspicion, to reduce the likelihood of being recognized."

"What will happen if that crazy one is allowed to continue to rule?" Martin asked himself as well as his brother. "I hope that the German people prove themselves in the end," he said, and his facial expression was a mixture of hope and worry.

"When the intellectuals start to support him, then we will really be in trouble," said Max.

"I don't believe it will come to that," said Martin.

Before Dr. Klopstock was unceremoniously thrown out of the museum in Berlin, he took photographs of all the archeological materials he had at his disposal, and he used these to continue his research during his time in hiding. When his brother came upon Martin engrossed in his work he asked,

"Is someone paying you to do this?"

Martin looked at Max and answered, "I hope that one day someone will compensate me for it."

His brother's look was a combination of repugnance and admiration when he said, "You hope, do you?"

Martin had spent much time thinking about Thutmose. Over the long period of time during which he formed his opinions about the ancient statue, warm admiration had grown in his heart toward this great man. However, recently there had been the beginnings of an erosion of sorts of his appreciation for Thutmose, and he found himself having conflicting thoughts about him. Thutmose had tried to convince himself and the world that his affair with Nefertiti had begun only after she had lost the faithfulness of her husband who had abandoned her in favor of sexual relations with the younger woman, Kiya. This is what Martin had believed as well when he built Thutmose up in his imagination as an admirable character. Lately, however, so much evidence had come to light from Martin's poring over the collection of materials in his drawers, that pointed to Nefertiti's betrayal of her husband with Thutmose having occurred a considerable time before Kiya became the woman in Akhenaton's arms.

This discovery came as a shock to Martin. It became clear that these two figures, to whom his admiration had assigned inhuman proportions, were actually stained and flawed people. For Martin, knowing of their betrayal brought them back into the realm of problematic humanity.

Martin told his brother about his conflicting thoughts concerning Nefertiti and Thutmose. Max responded with a rebuke. "Do you really think you can judge the behavior of a man and woman living in the Pharaoh's palace three thousand years ago under the conditions you described to me, by the standards of behavior we set for couples in a similar situation in our day?"

"Why not? What has changed since then? People are still the same as they were," said Martin.

"Everything has changed! Imagine if three thousand years ago the king had come into the studio where the artist was working on his statue of the queen, only to find his wife making love with another man. His anger would justify the immediate beheading of Thutmose. He could demand the head of his unfaithful wife also be cut from her shoulders, right before his eyes. Whereas today, in similar circumstances, Nefertiti would most likely say to her husband, "excuse me, please leave and close the door behind you, you are disturbing us," said Max. Unfortunately for Martin, his current situation left him plenty of free time in which to ruminate on the time of the Pharaohs. He had enough to also to reconstruct the events that he still did not completely understand.

Meanwhile, things were becoming grave for Martin and Max. The reports that came over the radio and were printed in the newspapers that they were able to attain, made it clear to the two brothers that the government's attitude toward the Jews was at its lowest ebb. The two families gradually reduced their outings to public places to only those times when absolutely necessary such as for buying bread or receiving or sending mail from the post office. Keeping up any communication with the outside world put them in danger because of the name Klopstock, which they had not changed.

One day the media announced that the government of Egypt was demanding that the Germans return the bust of Queen Nefertiti. The bust had been discovered by a German archeologist and had been illegally removed from Egypt. The bust was then located at the Berlin Museum. There immediately appeared a chain of articles reminding the German people, who were great lovers of culture and the arts, how much their good taste had improved after exposure to inspirational works of art. The articles mentioned the Germans' love of rare works, and in particular their affinity for the art of ancient times.

The Fuhrer made a special radio broadcast in which he told the enlightened nation that so supported the arts, that the bust of Queen Nefertiti was dear to the poetic soul of every German. After this speech the bust turned into a spiritual symbol for every Arian man and woman worthy of the name. The newspapers printed photographs of the bust of the most beautiful woman in the world. The name Nefertiti means "the beautiful woman has arrived", and this is what was told to a nation that never stopped teaching or learning. Marlene Dietrich was a bit insulted, and the reputations of several other beautiful German women were damaged. But – that was the Fuhrer's opinion. He said as much and his words were accepted with understanding and support.

Martin said to Max, "Now it's clear what direction this regime is headed. And it is not a good one. We can expect some very bad days ahead. The nation loves its Fuhrer."

Max responded with cynicsm, "You see Martin, even the Fuhrer, may his name be cursed, agrees with you that Nefertiti is the most beautiful woman in the world."

Martin did not respond to his brother's comment. He simply said, "Max, I am truly fearful about what the future will bring. From now on, we can expect only terrible surprises." Martin knew with certainty that the world was going from bad to worse.

The Fuhrer gave an order that had Martin been aware of, would have driven him out of his mind and perhaps would have put him in a life-threatening situation. The Fuhrer's order was that several copies be made of the bust of Nefertiti, so that when the time came to negotiate a settlement with the Egyptians, the Germans would retain the original sculpture.

Soon afterwards, the Second World War broke out. The German people were told that the British and French had betrayed them and had declared war on peace-seeking Germany. Later there were reports of victims – and these fallen early heroes were given huge funerals. It was later reported that the deaths of the brave German soldiers had been compensated when the German army soundly punished the criminal Poles.

Since they heard no reports regarding the fate of the Jews of the Third Reich, Max told Martin that perhaps the Fuhrer had decided to leave them alone. Martin assured him, however, that it would be quite a while before they could celebrate.

One night, loud knocking was heard on the doors of the two homes on Max's land. Both families were loaded onto trucks that immediately disappeared into the darkness. First the men were separated from their families, and soon afterwards Max was taken and removed from Martin's sight. Martin was transported to a concentration camp. He searched there for the members of his family, but could find not one of them. Some time later, Martin was transferred to a different concentration camp where he had more time left to his own devices. This camp held many younger men, and they had been told that for the time being they had been designated as laborers who would work in service to the Reich. One day a group of these young workers was loaded onto a rail car with no windows. They stood crowded together as the train covered a long distance. They were happy when the train finally came to a stop and they were ordered to jump down from the car. They all understood German, and jump they did – into an abandoned mine that had long since stopped being a source of iron. They were ordered to turn the mine pit into a series of rooms to be used for the production of weapons – a new kind of machine gun developed by the engineers of the Reich. Martin's group was responsible for manufacturing the various parts of the guns.

Nothing was ever told to them directly, but information whispered by those who had been there for a while would reach the ears of the newcomers. Martin had very little to eat and his weight plummeted, but he made the decision not to give up. He was a healthy man and he knew that no matter what hardships were in store, he would endure. The Nazi villains would not do him in. Martin worked in that mine for a period of about two and a half years.

One morning in their daily line-up, Martin's name was called as one of a group of men who were loaded onto a truck that transported them to a train. The train took its human cargo on a journey that ended at yet another mine – this one was an abandoned salt mine located in a place called Merkers Kieselbach, in Thuringia (one of the sixteen states of Germany). Apparently, Martin and his group were thought to be the prisoners most fit to work under the conditions of this mine, deep underground. The salt mine at Merkers Kieselbach had a special purpose. Here the Germans kept expensive works of art and the gold treasures they had robbed from their victims across Europe. Martin and the other men were charged with the task of enlarging the existing mine and getting it ready to receive additional shipments.

One day a rumor circulated in the mine that the bust of Queen Nefertiti, so loved by the Fuhrer, was to be delivered to the mine to be put under special protection. This delivery caused the salt mine to be one of the most to heavily secured areas under the Third Reich.

When Martin heard about this, his blood froze in his veins and his heart missed a beat. Fate had brought him close to the bust again, after he'd been torn away from it in the past. Martin knew that bust and its history better than any living person in the world. He could not help but think that it was the hand of God that brought it to be hidden in one of the wings of the mine, in such close proximity to him.

Martin thought, "Why would they bring the bust here? Does this mean the war is no longer progressing according to the plans of the Fuhrer? In Berlin there are many deep basements. The bust of Nefertiti must have been kept in one of them during the successful periods of the war, where it had been safe from any damage that might be inflicted during an enemy attack. The relocating of the bust to this mine must mean that the cellars of the museum in Berlin were no longer considered safe."

During the entire length of the war, Martin was completely cut off from what was happening in the world. He had lost his family and not even a shred of information came to him about their fate. He did not have even the most minimal information about the war during those years. For a long time he functioned only in the darkness, with no knowledge of the events unfolding in the world above the salt mine. The moving of Nefertiti to the mine was the first piece of information from which he could draw any conclusion about the course of those events.

Martin did everything in his power to obtain information about the location within the mine of the hiding place of the bust of Nefertiti, but the secret was well-kept and did not penetrate the network of whispers and rumors that fed the souls of the workers of the mine. This network served to squelch any hope in the hearts of the prisoners working in the unending darkness. Martin decided to invent the "Nefertiti Effect" in the mine. He spread the rumor that the arrival of Nefertiti to the mine signified that the end of the war was approaching. He also circulated the story of the "Curse of the Pharaohs".

The Nazi officers knew their task was to guard the secret of the bust of Nefertiti in the mine. From now on it would be clear to them that anyone who tried to touch the ancient queen would be die a miserable death caused by vicious microbes.

Martin had no access to actual facts on which to base his forecast that the war was about to end. The few words spoken now and again by the frightened German guards who oversaw his work did not contribute a lot of information. After hearing what Martin told them, they seemed to feel less secure. One of them even said that the cursed war was coming to an end and that he was happy about it. Martin felt it would be too dangerous for him to ask which side was winning, but he felt that the Nazi arrogance lately seemed to be lessoning, which encouraged him to increase his efforts to pass around his stories through the network of the mine.

One day Martin noticed that the guards were concealing their weapons. Some of them quickly changed from their uniforms into civilian clothing. A short time after this the mine area was suddenly filled with vehicles of an unfamiliar type. They were American Jeeps and they brought American soldiers and officers who swarmed the mine. Martin went among the Americans hugging and kissing them, one after the other. He whispered in each of their ears in Hebrew, *"Mi Sheberah"*, until one of the soldiers answered him, saying, *"Shema Yisrael"*. Hearing this, Martin could not control his emotions and wept out loud. Tears streamed down his own cheeks and wetted the face of the soldier who tightly embraced him.

Martin's English was not fluent, but he did know enough of the language to exchange a few sentences with the American soldier, Corporal Isaac Freulich. "Where are you from, Jew?" he asked, after gulping water from the soldier's canteen and reviving a little.

"From Brooklyn, New York," said Isaac as he continued to examine the face of the unfortunate Jew who stood before him.

Martine stared at the gun shouldered by his savior. He lifted his hand and stroked the weapon. He then mustered the strength to rise up on his toes and kiss the cold metal of the gun. His eyes began to tear again.

"Do you know a Jew in Brooklyn named Richard Klopstock?" he asked.

"Your relative?"

"Yes, my uncle. My father's brother."

"I'm sorry. I don't recall ever meeting a Jew by that name before the war. You know, there are quite a few Jews in Brooklyn," Isaac explained to Martin.

Suddenly an order rang out sharply in English. Isaac stood at attention and turned to look toward the entrance of the mine. A Jeep rolled slowly toward Isaac. Meanwhile floodlights had been aimed into largest room of the mine and Martin saw for the first time the proportions of the huge mine in which he had spent so many long months. The Jeep came to a stop and an officer with the rank of Major stood down from it. He examined the faces of Isaac and Martin. "The two stood next to one another, their faces wet with tears. The officer turned to Isaac. "Corporal", he said, "I see that you have made a connection with this man."

"Yes, sir." Isaac answered.

"Does he speak English?"

"Not much, but enough," was Isaac's response.

"Ask him what he and the others need. Food, water, blankets, cigarettes?"

Martin looked at the officer. He seemed to understand the meaning of the instructions being given to Isaac. Martin marched up to the officer, fell to his knees and told him in halting English, "God bless you."

The officer was moved, lost his decorum for a moment, and out of habit he removed his metal hat. When he recovered, returning his helmet to his head, he strode the few steps to where Martin stood, bent toward him, and with his strong arms, stood him back up. "Nobody kneels before an American officer, sir," he told him. After a short pause he asked, "where did you learn English?"

Martin was confused by the simplicity of the question and he gave a more involved answer, "In school, at work, at the museum, from reading, studying for my doctorate."

Isaac's commanding officer did not understand every word of the answer but his impression was that there stood before him an educated man, now a mere shadow of himself, still finding it within him to function like a human being. He shot out an order to Isaac. "Take this man and put him in the Jeep."

"Yes, Major Chester," Isaac hurried to carry out the order, supporting Martin and assisting him to get situated in the back seat.

"Try to find out from him where the office of the commander of the mine is," said the Major to Isaac as he opened up a map that seemed to be a diagram of the mine. Martin understood the question. He pointed with his hand and the Major began to drive the vehicle in that direction. The officer did not have to put forth much effort. The Lieutenant Colonel who was commander of the mine and his officers stood at attention outside the entrance to the office.

The Major got down from his car, nodded his head toward Martin and said in English "Tell this officer that I wish to have given to me immediately all of the maps of the mine."

Martin gathered all of his strength. He turned to the Lieutenant Colonel and told him, in German, "The American commander demands that you give him all of the maps of the mine, immediately."

"The German officer remained in place, tapping his boot, and answered: "Tell the commander that in order to give him the maps I will have to go into the office."

Martin translated the German commander's answer. Behind them, meanwhile, another Jeep had pulled up in which sat junior officers. The American Major turned to the captain sitting at the steering wheel and told him to go into the office and receive all of the blueprints of the mine from the German officer. The Major then looked at Martin: "The German commander must go into the office and give all he has to the Captain." He pointed to the Captain.

Upon receiving this instruction from Martin the German officer responded with "Jawohl!" and hurried to enter the office. He went to a file cabinet and pulled out large files containing charts and diagrams. The American captain stood next to him. Martin tried to get down off the Jeep in order to help with translating their conversation, but his body's meager strength would not allow him to do what he wished and he stayed seated on the Jeep. The Major saw this and told Isaac, "Corporal, there is no need for him to get up, keep an eye on him and perhaps get him some water to drink."

Martin looked at Isaac and said, "Tell your commander that before the war I worked in a museum in Berlin on the bust of Nefertiti, which the Nazis are now hiding here, at the mine."

Isaac did not understand what Martin was telling him but he understood that he was trying to relay something on a matter of great importance.

"Sir," Isaac addressed the Major, "I think this man has something important to tell you."

"What about?" asked the Major.

"Please repeat what you said," Isaac told Martin.

"Nefertiti, Nefertiti, here in the mine," Martin raised his voice as much as he could as he spoke to the Major.

"The American commander jumped into action and hurried up to Isaac asking: "What is he saying about Nefertiti?" It was obvious from his reaction that this name was engraved clearly on his consciousness. Isaac did not understand the meaning of the word Nefertiti. It didn't sound like a German name, and his ability to help in the matter was limited. But Martin saw the Major's instant reaction and he repeated himself in the best English he could manage: "The bust of Nefertiti is here, in the mine." As he said this Martin, pointed downward with his thumb.

The American Major understood the gist of what Martin said. He jumped down off his Jeep, went into the office and spread out a map of the mine. He turned to the German commander and said, "Nefertiti."

The German understood the question. He took one step toward the map, examined it, and placed his finger on a particular spot.

"Come with me" said the Major to the German commander, and getting into the Jeep with Martin he repeated: "Nerfertiti." The German commander nodded his head. "Follow us" shouted the Major to the captain in the Jeep behind them. They stopped in front of a locked room jutting out from the wall of the mine. The German commander took a bunch of keys from his pocket and opened the door. With a wave of his hand he lighted the dark room. Everyone stood motionless, facing a still wooden box.

With the last of his strength, Martin heaved himself

from the Jeep. He tried to walk but could not. Isaac hurried to hold him up. Martin went into the room, where he fell down again and began to cry bitterly. He tried to move toward the large wooden box that leaned against the wall. He wanted to wrap his arms around it. But he was blocked by a transparent barrier that was in his way. A thick shield of glass stood between the box and the group of men standing in front of it. Through the glass they could clearly read the name "Nefertiti". It was written on the box in large letters.

The American officers, Isaac, and the German officers stood in a semi-circle around Martin and the box, gazing with wonderment at the vision before their eyes.

"Corporal, help him get up," ordered the Major when he saw that Martin tried without success to rise from his knees.

Martin turned to Isaac and said, "please tell your commander that I am an archeologist and that I worked on this bust of Nefertiti before the war in a museum in Berlin. I do not wish to be parted from her again." Isaac understood that the box contained something important having to do with Martin's past and he tried to relay that information to his commander.

Everyone was evacuated from the mine. The German commanders were taken into custody and investigation, and the prisoners who had worked the mines, Martin among them, were taken to field hospitals that were set up nearby. The Major put a guard in front of the entrance to the mine and he set up security all around its perimeter since he suspected there were other entrances to the place that he hoped yet to discover.

Two days later, a commotion went up around the salt mine at Merkers Kieselbach, in Thuringia. Earlier, a rumor had been circulated in April, 1945, that General Dwight D. Eisenhower, Commander in Chief of the Allied Forces in the European theater, was going to visit the region. He indeed arrived, and accompanied by the officers from his international headquarters, he toured the underground halls that contained huge collections of art treasures as well as large stores of gold guided by Major Chester, who ended the tour by bringing them to the hidden room where Nefertiti's famous bust was kept inside its wooden box. He explained to General Eisenhower the great importance the Fuhrer had place upon this three thousand year old Egyptian sculpture, the capture of which by the Americans sealed their winning of the cultural side of the war.

That same day General Eisenhower also paid a visit to the liberated prisoners at the hospital where they were receiving care. Major Chester introduced Martin Klopstock to the general, explaining that the Doctor was an archeologist who in the past had done much work on the bust of Nefertiti until Hitler came to power and he was prevented from continuing his research. Further, he told the General, Martin apparently had more expertise in the subject than anyone in the world. It was certainly a great irony that Dr. Klopstock had been sent by the

Nazis to work in the very salt mine where they hid the famous bust of Nefertiti. The General was very impressed by what Major Chester told him. He wanted to know more about Martin Klopstock, and requested that they meet when Martin recovered and regained his strength.

When Martin heard that General Eisenhower had taken an interest in him, he formulated two requests that he would make of him. First, he wanted to know what had become of his family and that of his brother, Max. Second, he wanted to return as soon as possible, along with the bust of Nefertiti, to the Berlin Museum and to resume his work where he had left off in 1933.

Three weeks after Martin made his requests, he received a response from General Eisenhower's office. To the General's great sorrow, none of the names of Martin's family members appeared on the lists of survivors, but they were not giving up and the matter would continue to be investigated. As for the second request, the possibility of bringing the bust back to Berlin had been looked at, but because of the destruction in the area of the museum, it was decided that the move would be delayed until a later time.

In addition, Martin was told that even though Potsdam had sustained extensive damage, Martin's house was intact and he could return there whenever he was ready, with the help of the American army. Martin requested to return to his hometown immediately, and that request was fulfilled.

A family had been given Martin's house as a give from the Nazi party in thanks for special services to the Third Reich. They left the house hastily after receiving a surprise visit from an American intelligence officer demanding that they show a deed to the house. When they produced the documents given them by the Nazi party, the officer confiscated them and told the family to find a good lawyer, preferably a Jewish one, because they were about to be called to trial on charges of taking possession of the house illegally. The head of the household was not present as he had been killed a year earlier on the eastern front, but his wife understood what she needed to do, and by the time Martin arrived at his house, it was empty.

Martin found that the squatters had left the house in good condition. It was clean and orderly, and the furnishings had barely been changed at all. Once he was settled into his old home Martin devoted all of his time to his efforts at locating any traces of the missing members of his family. He visited Max's two farms, where he and his family and his brother's family had been rounded up and taken, but he found no information there. General Eisenhower's people also found nothing additional to help him.

A short time after Martin's return to Potsdam, the city underwent a transformation that changed the rules of the game.

One morning Martin became aware of a commotion going on around Potsdam. Military vehicles flying the flags of the United States, Great Britain, and the Soviet Union were traversing the city in all directions. Martin saw that most of the activity centered around the Cecilienhof palace. The Cecilienhof was the last palace built by the Hohenzollern family during the period when Potsdam was the capitol of the Kingdom of Prussia. It was named after the wife of the heir apparent, Wilhelm, who received the palace as a gift from his father, Wilhelm II, in 1917. Martin knew the palace well from his student days when he had made his living as a guide. It had been an important stop on his itinerary, during which he would explain to the tourists that the occupants of the palace had not had a very long time in which to enjoy it. In November 1918, following the military defeat of Germany in the First World War and the German Revolution, the family was forced to leave Germany and to relocate in Holland. In 1926 the government of the Weimar Republic returned the palace to the prince's family after Wilhelm gave up his right to the throne, but in 1945, as the Red Army closed in on Potsdam, the family was again forced to leave the palace and escape to western Germany.

Martin quickly figured out why there was so much bustling about at the Cecilienhof palace. The palace was the site of a meeting between the Big Three which began on August 2, 1945. For two weeks they hashed out the new international agreements that defined control of Europe at the end of World War II. The result of the Potsdam Conference seemed to be that Josef

Stalin received almost everything he demanded. He was the only one of the Big Three who had participated world leadership conferences prior to this, and he played upon the weaknesses of the two other leaders. At the outset of the conference Britain was represented by Winston Churchill, who had lead them through the war and understood all of the ins and outs, but during the conference the British replaced him with Clement Attlee, the Labour party leader who had just become Prime Minister and had no experience dealing with the stuff that Stalin was made of. President Harry Truman represented the Americans at the conference, taking the place of the late President Franklin Delano Roosevelt. Most of his focus was on the continuing struggle in the Pacific Ocean against the Japanese, and he tried to get Stalin's agreement to a military invasion inside Japanese territory and to dropping an atom bomb on Hiroshima or another city in Japan.

Like the rest of the curious citizens, Martin tried to find out what was happening at the palace that had become a zone of the highest security known to the world at that time. He was concerned about his family, about the fate of the rest of the Jewish survivors of the war, and about the world at large. What was to become of Europe? There were very few Jews in the vicinity of the Cecilienhof palace during the time of the Potsdam Conference. Martin feared being taken into custody by the Allied military police for being a German with no papers. He thought his presence in that particular place might arouse suspicions that he had undesirable intentions. His mostly feared the Soviets, who showed an especially strong tendency toward taking revenge on the Germans for crimes against the Soviet people.

During the time directly after the end of the war, German intellectuals had not yet begun to complain that the Allies in general and the Soviets in particular, were punishing the Germans with untoward cruelty. Those intellectuals who had survived were busy with trying to find food for themselves and their households, and had not the leisure to pursue the argument that many of the bombs that had fallen on their cities were in the name of revenge rather than real military strategy on the part of the Allies.

Martin became caught up in thoughts and emotions. He was happy that Germany, his birthplace, had suffered a bitter defeat in the war, but it was a source of sorrow for him to see the way Potsdam, his hometown, had been destroyed. He had not yet gone back to Berlin. He very much wanted to visit the museum where he'd worked before the Nazis sent him away, but he felt that it was not yet time.

Right after the Potsdam Conference ended and the results were announced, Martin read in the newspaper that one of the decisions that had been taken there was that Germany was to be divided into zones of occupation, and to each of the four powers would be given exclusive authority over one zone. Potsdam was in the zone to be controlled by the Soviets. This development came as shock to Martin. He immediately decided that he must once again leave his home and move to the part of Berlin that was under the authority of the United States. He feared that the British would rule with a tough hand in response to their cities, London in particular, having been brutally bombarded by Göring and his pilots during the war.

Martin remained one last night in his house. The next morning he would say goodbye, likely forever, to the place the Klopstocks had called home for generations. Martin knew that if he tried to sell his house it was likely to bring only a small amount, since so few people would be willing to invest in a home located in the area under Soviet control. Furthermore trying to sell would require him to stay on for a time, and he feared that the Soviets might soon close the area, which would leave him trapped in the Soviet zone of occupation. This risk he was not willing to take. Max's farms were also in the Soviet area, and so were of no help to him. He visited the homes there, and although they had not been damaged by the Allied bombs, they looked abandoned and neglected. The farms were likely to soon be occupied by families who had supported the Soviet war effort, since there was clearly a need for agricultural products and food.

Martin went to Berlin and found a penthouse apartment only slightly damaged by the bombings. The apartment owner showed him that it still had running water and a working sewage system. He knew he could restore what was left of the apartment to a reasonable space for himself that would provide him shelter for the near future. Of course, there was still the question of earning a living. Isaac, the Jewish-American soldier, had loaned him one hundred dollars. Though not a small amount, it was almost used up.

Martin faced a difficult dilemma. In Berlin he met with a Jewish Agency worker who had come from the Land of Israel. This clerk tried to help him, and suggested that he apply to "go up" to Palestine. There was a very good reason for him to accept this offer. It was there that the list of survivors was being organized. The clerk told Martin that if any of his family members were still alive, they would likely have been brought to Palestine, and that by going there he would have the best chance of finding them. Martin did not know about the conflict between the British Mandatory authority and the Jewish community or how Jews were being prevented from going to Palestine.

After weighing all of this, in his heart Martin still felt that his decision not to leave Germany was the right one. In spite of all that had happened, he would remain. He would wait until the museum in Berlin reopened and return to resume his work on the bust of Nefertiti. He was sure that he would be re-hired to that job.

In any case, in his pocket he kept Isaac's address. He had not written to him since his arrival in Potsdam but he would write to him as soon as he had a permanent address in Berlin, in order to keep the communication between them open. As soon as he was settled in his Berlin apartment he set out to look for work. He was certain that construction workers would be needed for the restoration of the museum, and he wanted to be among them, so as to work in proximity to the museum and keep an eye on what developed there.

Chapter Eleven:
Nevertheless

S pread in front of him on the table were photos of family members that Martin had found at the farm when he visited. The photos were of his wife Clara and their two sons, Gustav and Karl. He looked at his wife's face and thought about how much she resembled Nefertiti. They had similar serious, yet dreamy expressions that barely concealed the hint of a smile, much like Leonardo Da Vinci's Mona Lisa. Nefertiti had dark hair and eyes, while Clara's eyes were light and her hair blond. This was almost the only difference between the two that Martin was able to discern. Of course it was difficult to be sure of the color of Nefertiti's hair since the large turban she wore on her head covered it up, a turban thought of as a crown in her day. Her eyebrows were dark, however.

Then Martin discovered another difference. Clara's lips were meatier than Nefertiti's. It was unclear from whom in Clara's family history she had inherited such lips. Martin felt a deep dejection come over him. He blamed himself for having been occupied with thoughts of Nefertiti and of Clara, both of them appearing in his daydreams often, whereas his sons were absent from those visions. He could not even remember how they looked. A heavy guilt lay over his heart and it affected him physically, making his movements clumsy.

Six years had passed since the merciless Nazis had separated them. For the first time since his loved ones had been torn from him, he allowed all of his thoughts to be centered upon them. What had been their fate? Could they still be alive? How would they look today? Would he recognize them? He felt the need to consult with a therapist – someone who might guide him in dealing with the present reality. Now that the threat of immediate death that was his constant companion during the war years was removed, it's place was taken by the question of continuity. Survival. How? What for? Theoretically, he knew that sooner or later he would go back to Nefertiti, but would he have the inner strength necessary to continue his research? Would he really be accepted, or would he experience what had happened to many other scientists who tried to become close to her? The most recent of them had looked at her for just a few seconds and then turned their attention to other works of art. They formed no commitment toward her.

With this question, he turned his thoughts back to Clara. He suddenly felt that if only he and Clara could be together again, he would find the strength to continue his research on Nefertiti. "That is a crazy thought," he told himself. Why would he think that Carla's support would pave the way for him to Nefertiti? After all, the two women were rivals!

Suddenly he had a thought. Did the Nefertiti of his past still really exist? Twelve years had gone by since he had seen her last. Meanwhile a terrible war had taken place that had brought about the loss of his family and of a third of his body's mass. Perhaps he had undergone neurological changes as well as a result of what he had experienced.

Martin did not even consider in all of this his sensitive nature that had driven his behavior even before the onset of the war. His boss at the museum, Dr. Katzelbaum, had once told him, "I need you here because you are a scientist with the soul of an artist." At the time Martin had thought those words were spoken frankly and out of kindness. A short time later, when Martin came to work one morning, Dr. Katzelbaum said, "Martin, starting tomorrow morning someone else will be taking your place in this office. I'm sorry. Orders." And with that, Martin's work with Nefertiti had ended.

Since then, Martin had no contact whatever with her. Each night Martin thought about her, and about Clara. He thought about his sons as well, but less. He felt his eyes closing. He felt exhausted. Could he be losing his vitality?

A telegram arrived. Martin had forgotten that letters could be sent and received speedily. Ever since the Nazis had come to power he had ceased to use this form of communication. Maybe it had come by mistake? The telegram was sent by Schmulik, the Jewish Agency clerk, and it contained a request to call him as soon as possible. Martin wondered what the Jewish Agency wanted to discuss with him about his leaky apartment in Berlin. He read the paper in his hand again. Suddenly his whole body began to shake. He remembered Gustav, Karl, and Clara. "Could it be?" he heard himself shout.

"I'm sorry, but we have heard nothing about Gustav, but Clara Klopstock and Karl Klopstock appear on our list. They are in an absorption center in Amsterdam."

Schmulik offered Martin a chair, and he fell into it. Schmulik continued to explain how they had been located, but Martin heard nothing except "Amsterdam, Amsterdam, Amsterdam". Finally he forced out the words, "When will I see them?"

"Do you think you are able to make the trip to Amsterdam?"

Martin felt his strength returning and answered, "I am able to travel to the North Pole!"

"Excellent," answered Schmulik, encouraged by the change he saw come over Martin. He tried several times to dial the telephone that stood on his desk, and finally made a connection. "Your son, Karl," Schmulik said and handed Martin the receiver.

"Karl," he shouted.

"Papa," he heard.

Their voices were muffled by the streams of their tears.

"Have you hear anything about Gustav?" he asked, bringing father and son back to reality.

"No Papa, I haven't."

"Are you alright?"

"Yes, Papa."

"Is your mother there with you?"

"Yes, Papa."

"Let me speak to her, please."

"Of course."

"Clara?"

There was noise on the other end of the line."

"Clara, I am waiting for you to answer me."

"Martin," he finally heard a soft whisper.

"How are you?" he asked.

There was silence.

"Are you alright?"

"Yes."

"Schmulik from the Jewish Agency will tell me how to get to you on the train. I will arrive tomorrow," said Martin.

"Good," Clara answered in a voice choked with sobs.

The last twelve years of Martin's life had been filled with much sorrow and anguish. They had taught him to what unimaginable proportions the evil of man could reach, and only a bit about human compassion. He had learned that when negotiating among the many possible traps that lay between good and evil, he must not make mistakes, especially no gross mistakes. It was good that he had abandoned the house in Potsdam and moved to Berlin. From the stories he heard about the behavior of the Soviet soldiers it was clear that he would not have wanted to fall into their hands. Schmulik suggested that now he might want to reconsider traveling to the Land of Israel. He called it "going up". But Martin still wanted to stay in Germany. Perhaps Karl would want to seek his fortune in Palestine. He could decide for himself. He might go there after finishing his university studies. They would talk about that. Would his apartment be large enough for the three of them, and perhaps a fourth if they could locate Gustav as well?

And Clara - would they be able to adjust to this new life? She surely had experienced her own hell during the war. She may have lost her freshness and beauty. He would try to treat her with patience and consideration. In the past they had argued often. She had called him a stubborn husband and father with a Prussian personality. And she had been right. He regretted the many mistakes he had made in the past. Perhaps he would not make them now, when he and Clara made a new start. Martin assumed that the war years had wrung from Clara all of the jealousy and hatred she had felt toward Nefertiti. At least he hoped so.

They moved to a different apartment, a bit larger and less leaky. Martin's weight slowly came back, as did his strength. He needed a lot of physical stamina for his work in the construction and rebuilding of the destroyed buildings of Berlin. Meanwhile, they were informed that Gustav would not return, that he had been cut off from this world with vicious cruelty. Karl decided that he would not build his home in a country where such things had occurred. He joined a group of young people who "went up" to Israel in order to establish a new kind of community - one with high standards, built by "Yekkim" (German immigrants to Israel), based on the principles of justice and equality.

He left behind parents who had to try to start their lives over again.

Martin went back to thinking his thoughts and dreaming his dreams from before the war. To his amazement he found that this was not difficult. He compared the strength he required to do his construction work with what it must have taken for the ancient Egyptian laborers to withstand their crushing working conditions. Ror, at the beginning of his career must surely have been a much stronger and more muscular man than Martin, who would never have been able survive the quarry, much less have risen to the heights that Ror did. The museum director informed him that the building restoration would continue for many years. In the meantime all of the exhibits were moved into the part of the building that still stood at Schloss Charlottenburg in Berlin. Perhaps soon he would be called to do archeological work, and might even be able to start over where he left off in 1933.

Martin and Clara were not able to return to the point where they had been before the war broke out. Several years passed, and he did return to his previous occupation. They made a concerted effort to recover their relationship, but it remained uncertain that they could mend the tears that had resulted from their long separation.

The love from the days of their youth drew its last breath and their remaining joy in life dissolved when they heard they had lost Gustav. Martin read an article on "mature love", written by a Polish psychologist and translated into German. The article said that love is an eternal fire that can never be extinguished – a flame that burns until the end of life. Martin wondered whether these statements were a result of the author's professional observations or an expression of her opinions based on her personal life experience. He asked Clara for her opinion on the eternal flame of love. Clara responded that she had not yet reached an age at which she could answer with certainly to what extent that was true. He felt that Clara had not given the matter enough thought. He doubted that she had taken into account her previous hatred of Nefertiti, which must certainly have an influence on her feelings for him.

Martin whispered to Clara, "I feel more thirsty for love than ever. Now that we are alone together, what is the point of living if there is no love between us?" And at that moment Nefertiti was the farthest thing from his mind.

"You are right. Now I appreciate every bit of goodness that I see. Starting with the morning sun, and until the moon dances around us at night. I don't see the bad things – they simply pass before my eyes and disappear. In the past, that wasn't true. I always had to be in two places at once. I was angry about things that never happened, and about promises that were never kept. You were always at work when I needed you. The way we lived when we were young made you see the blue in the color green, while I saw the yellow. We each insisted that we were right. We ignored the fact that green contains both the yellow and the blue, and so we fought. Each of us stood stubbornly in defense of our own lonely color. And when we made up, I would start to see the red in the violet and you would see the blue, and so our arguments would continue. Today we both refuse to play forbidden games of optical blending that emphasize the color differences that could exacerbate the conflicts between us. On the contrary, we value our lack of divisiveness," said Clara.

"You are right, Clara, in our youth, in our excitement to squeeze out all that we thought we deserved in life, we built ourselves barriers that now we know were unnecessary," answered Martin.

Each of them brought clear intention to the new reality, and they functioned with the cooperation necessary to create the harmony they desired. Without clear intention and ambition to rise to new heights together, they would not have the ability to carry out their intentions.

Gustav, who was no longer with them and would never return, was in their thoughts. all the time, and he always would be. They talked about what they had all shared during the days before the war and decided not to talk about Gustav in the past tense, though the decision was never voiced in words. Glances between them expressed their intention. They were like a remnant left after the fires of the inferno. Survival gave them life and a future.

When the time came for Clara to move on from this life, letting go of his wife was very hard for Martin. In the last years of their lives together they had formed the strong companionship and bond that many couples aspire to. It was a love made up of conciliation, consensus, compromise, and cooperation. Martin no longer concerned himself with Nefertiti and the competition between the two women disappeared as if it had never been. Only Clara remained, with Martin at her side. Actually, Clara's jealousy of Nefertiti had become more moderate years before it finally disappeared. When Clara discovered that the resemblance between them was so amazingly exact, she had calmed considerably. She had come to understand that her husband, Martin, projected her qualities onto Nefertiti, and that his love for Nefertiti was really another expression of his love for her, Clara. He borrowed not only her outward appearance but also her personality. Her passion for physical love, he found in that woman. Through his wife he experienced the jealousy that Nefertiti had felt, and he recognized the feminine pride exhibited by the Egyptian queen. He saw Clara's argumentativeness in Nefertiti as well. The ancient beauty had liked to sip apricot nectar, and Clara enjoyed wine – especially the Kaiser Schtoll. They both had a tendency to get a bit drunk – Nefertiti by taking just a sip followed by another sip of narcotic flower extracts, and Clara imbibing a less addicting substance, imported whisky. It is clear that Clara was not precise in her comparison, but she felt comfortable making it, and in this she attained a personal peace with Martin.